ZODIAC

SIXTH

🐟 *(February 20 — March 20)*

Other worldly, intelligent Pisces is a dreamer. She can be like a psychic sponge and will know secret things about people which can be very disconcerting. Pisces is incredibly generous as well as being highly empathic and receptive with humans and animals.

Phoebe has inherited 'the gift' from her Cajun grandmother, which enables her to heal and help people. But these psychic powers also warn Phoebe of danger and treachery, which in turn lead her into dangerous waters from which she may not return.

ZODIAC

*Whatever your sun sign, you'll want to read
Zodiac, the series written in the stars.*

SERIES CREATED BY JAHNNA N. MALCOLM

ZODIAC

PISCES

SIXTH
SENSE

JAHNNA N. MALCOLM

Lions
An Imprint of HarperCollinsPublishers

First published in Lions in 1995

Lions is an imprint of CollinsChildren'sBooks,
a Division of HarperCollins*Publishers* Ltd,
77-85 Fulham Palace Road, Hammersmith, London W6 8JB

1 3 5 7 9 8 6 4 2

ISBN: 0 00 675046 X

Printed and bound in Great Britain by
HarperCollins Manufacturing Ltd, Glasgow.

To those terrific kids:
Matt L., Matt D., Montana, and Shiloh

CHAPTER ONE

PISCES (February 20 – March 20)
Transiting Saturn has put quite a damper on
your spirits. Your ruling planet, Neptune,
has shown you that dreams and harsh
reality are a difficult mix. Your vision for
the future is a little foggy right now, with
the past conjuring up tensions that want to
control the present. Just "let it be".

"*P*hoebe! Help me!"

The terror in her little brother's voice cut
through the morning air. Phoebe instantly
pulled her mind away from the herbs she was
gathering and looked back at the spot where
Shiloh had been standing only moments
before.

The sun was just beginning to slant
through the tupelo gum and cypress trees

lining both sides of the bayou, but there was already plenty of light to see that Shiloh was not nearby.

Phoebe Arceneaux spun in a circle, looking for Shiloh. The backwaters of a Louisiana bayou was no place for a five-year-old to be off on his own. It was barely a place for a seventeen-year-old.

Bayou country lay in the Southern part of the state along the Mississippi River delta and the Gulf of Mexico. Phoebe's family, members of the tightknit Cajun community, had lived along the swampy inlets for generations, fishing and trapping. These descendants of eighteenth century French-Canadians had found their way to this tiny pocket of the United States and lived in relative isolation for hundreds of years.

She glanced toward the *pirogue*, but the small canoe was still tied up at the side of the bank. Sluggish and dark green, the water looked tranquil. An alligator moving through it would have left ripples.

The thought almost turned her stomach. *Shiloh is OK. You just heard him scream. And he'll be lost only a moment more.*

"Phoebe!"

Fixing the direction in her mind, she dropped the basket of freshly picked swamp lily root and *l'mauve*. "Shiloh, where are you?" Phoebe ran through the thick forest, holding her dress in one fist to clear her legs. Her thick blonde plait thumped against her shoulders as she ran.

"Phoebe! I'm scared!"

A trio of blackbirds exploded out of a lightning-seared cypress dripping Spanish moss in front of her. The path was narrow and uneven. Blackberry brambles scratched at her from both sides.

Her brother lay flat on the ground, a small Easter basket full of plants overturned beside him. His foot was trapped in a tangle of roots from a nearby tree.

Shiloh's tawny blond hair fell into his face as he stared forward. His glasses lay on the ground beside him.

"Phoebe!" he wailed again. Phoebe could see nothing to cause his terror. When he was little, Shiloh used to insist he saw bears behind their house and would go to great lengths to describe how long and sharp their teeth were.

"Shiloh, you scared me half to death," Phoebe muttered. "I can't believe you'd pull a stunt like this."

When her father had asked her to gather some herbs for her grandmother before school, Phoebe had protested, but when he insisted that she took her little brother along, she had been absolutely livid. Now, once again, Shiloh was pretending to be hurt. Phoebe didn't have time for this. "Come on. We're going to be late for school."

"Snake!" Shiloh rasped. "There's a snake, Phoebe! Don't let it bite me!"

Phoebe suddenly froze. Not half a metre away a cottonmouth faced Shiloh, curled protectively round a dead toad. The snake's head was up, its mouth open, exposing the whitish-pink gums that gave the deadly creature its name. Over a metre long, dark olive brown in color, the cottonmouth was one of the biggest she'd ever seen.

"Oh my god." She swallowed hard and

took a cautious step forward. "Shiloh, I want you to listen to me. OK?"

"It's going to bite me," her brother wailed. "It'll hurt. It's all your fault. You weren't watching me. You should have been watching me, Phoebe. Mama told you to watch me."

The snake moved in response, coiling to strike.

"Don't move," Phoebe commanded. "Shiloh, it won't bite you as long as you listen to me." She hoped that was true.

"OK." He whimpered but remained still.

She looked round for a stick or a rock to try to scare the snake away. There was nothing close by. It was unlikely Shiloh would stay put if she had to retreat to get one.

Phoebe took another step forward, coming down on her knee beside Shiloh. She placed a hand on her brother's back and squeezed his shoulder reassuringly.

The reptile's gaze was cold as it met hers.

She heard her grandmother's voice in the back of her head. *"You have the gift, cher. It be in you, ain't no denying. 'Cept by you. You the only one can keep it locked up."*

"Go away," Phoebe said firmly to the snake. "There's no one here who wants to take your dirty old toad." She tried to make those thoughts strong. She concentrated totally on the cottonmouth, mentally sending it packing.

Granmere was able to do that. Once, when Mr Carbonnet's bird-dogs kept getting into the Duplantier family's henhouse, Mr Carbonnet had asked Granmere to talk to his dogs and make them stop because family feuds among the hot-blooded Cajun community had started over less.

Phoebe had gone with her, as part of her education in what her grandmother called "the old ways". The dogs had been rowdy and jumped all over the place. Granmere had sung a child's nursery song to the dogs, who were snarling – and it had been like magic. Granmere talked to them like small boys, telling them how bad they'd been. The dogs never went back to the henhouse again.

"You're a bad snake," she told the cottonmouth. "Go away. Now!" She felt a tightness in her chest and the world seemed to slow down round her. It was like that when Granmere said her gift was trying to surface inside her. Instead of being afraid of it, Phoebe clung to the feeling and tried to find the strength in it.

The snake closed its mouth and retreated slightly, hugging the dead toad.

"It worked!" Phoebe cried in disbelief. But her concentration slipped just as Shiloh tried to push himself up with one hand.

Without warning, the cottonmouth struck, lunging at her little brother with its bright, sharp fangs extended.

Before she could stop to think, Phoebe reached out and grabbed the snake behind the head in mid-strike. She didn't know who was more surprised – her, Shiloh, or the cottonmouth.

"Throw it away, Phoebe!" Shiloh shrilled. "Throw the snake away!"

The cottonmouth's skin felt smooth and cold as it tried to wrap round Phoebe's arm. Her breath frozen in her lungs, she flung the snake into the brush as hard as she could. It thrashed round angrily and then slithered away.

"Oh my god," Phoebe gasped as she bent down to help her little brother. "I can't believe I did that." Her hands shook as she freed Shiloh's foot from the tangled snarl of roots. She gathered him up and hugged him tightly.

"Phoebe, you did it!" Shiloh crowed. "You could be Superwoman!"

"C'mon, let's get out of here. That's enough excitement for one day." Phoebe took Shiloh by one hand and scooped up his glasses and Easter basket with the other.

"Wait'll I tell Mama and Papa," he cried.

Phoebe tried not to run back to the *pirogue*. As they walked, she kept glancing back for the cottonmouth, but she never saw it.

"I hope we see a 'gator on the way home," Shiloh babbled happily as he clambered aboard the *pirogue* with the agility of a monkey.

Phoebe untied the lines, pushed off, and stepped carefully into the boat. Normally she felt at home in the bayou. After all, she was a Pisces. Water was her element and the sea god Neptune her ruling planet. But today, as she put the pole into the water to push them out into the bayou, a sick feeling churned in her stomach and made her head feel as if it were going to burst.

At first she thought it was a reaction to the fright she'd just had. Then, with her head bent over the *pirogue's* edge, Phoebe saw shadowy images moving somewhere on the other side of the dark water.

She recognized the feeling. It was a premonition. Occasionally, when she looked into water, she saw things that came true. She didn't know what it was, but Phoebe knew something bad was about to happen. She grabbed the oars and rowed as hard as she could for home.

CHAPTER TWO

*T*he Arceneaux home stood on stilts above the flood level of Blackcat Bayou, where it had been for three generations. A thick copse of willow trees draped the structure, almost hiding it from casual view. The walls needed another coat of whitewash and a frayed rope held the tyre swing up from a tree in the front yard, but it was home.

Phoebe tied the *pirogue* up to the tall mast near the weathered boat dock. Shiloh scampered up the wooden ladder leading on to the dock. The water level had risen with the spring rains that had begun in March, but the climb up the ladder was still a steep one, especially with the herb baskets in one hand.

She followed the rise of the hill leading up to the house and found her mother standing inside the screened galley overlooking the bayou. Shiloh was regaling her with the morning's adventures.

"...an' it was this big," her little brother was saying, holding his hands as far apart as possible, "with big green teeth an' it wanted to bite my nose."

Normally a ruddy woman with a balanced outlook on life, Claire Arceneaux looked tense. Her hands constantly worked the dishtowel she held.

"Mama?" The cold from the premonition touched Phoebe again. "What's wrong?"

"Your granmere called," her mother answered, picking Shiloh up. "There's been some trouble at her house."

"Oh, no!" *The premonition. That's what it was about. Granmere!* "What happened?"

"I don't know. Papa's talking to her now."

Phoebe hurried into the house. Cluttered and cramped, the house smelled of fried fish, baked bread and pipe tobacco.

The kitchen was filled with a wood-burning stove, dishes, handmade cabinets with glass fronts, a refrigerator, and a free-standing stainless steel sink.

Cordell Arceneaux stood at the window in the kitchen, a tall, rawboned man darkly tanned from years of fighting the elements and hauling in fishing nets. His beard showed grey in it now, but his laugh was still a young man's. As usual, he was dressed in jeans, a T-shirt, and steel-toed boots that had taken everything the bayou could throw at them.

"You wait there, Mama," he said into the phone as he gazed out through the windows. The breeze ruffled his longish hair. "Them sheriff's deputies, that's what they be for. You ain't no spring chicken no more. You wait till they get there. Me, I'm leaving now." He hung up.

"What's wrong?" Phoebe asked.

"Your granmere's OK, girl," he said in his deep voice. His dark eyes flashed anger. "But trouble, there's been some of that. Get your school things and lunch and we go check on her before we get you to school, eh?"

Phoebe hurried. Gathering her schoolbag, she checked herself briefly in her mirror. *My god, Phoebe, you look like a swamp girl.*

She groaned in frustration. Facing down cottonmouths was much more preferable than walking into the halls of Port Charmant High looking like this. She undid her plait and ran a brush through her long blonde hair, trying to get some of the leaves out. Phoebe's skin was tanned and smooth from her Acadian heritage. Her most remarkable feature was her eyes, cerulean blue under dark brows that she had always thought were too thick. What made them so unusual was the shape of her pupils – not round, but perfect half-moons.

"She has the eyes of a cat," her mother had announced proudly to all of her friends. "It runs in our family."

"Girl," her father called from the front room. "Let's be about it. Them crawfish, they ain't gonna wait on me. And school, she's not gonna slow down none for you neither."

"Coming."

Her father was waiting in the living room, his shotgun clutched in a hard-knuckled fist. He led her out the door, pausing briefly to kiss her mother.

They took her father's joe boat. Powered by an outboard motor, the flat-bottomed craft would skim across the bayou. She sat in the prow and tucked her books under her seat. Nets filled the middle of the boat.

The outboard motor sputtered only a moment, then levelled off to a high-pitched buzz-saw noise. Her father brought the boat round expertly. They sped up the bayou, leaving white caps trailing in the brownish water.

Spray kicked up into Phoebe's face and she knew her hair was going to be a tangled mess. Grimly she clung to the railing and hoped that her grandmother was all right.

Abruptly, swinging wide round Hatton's Bend, they nearly smashed into a black Cris-Craft rocketing down the bayou. Her father acted instantly, avoiding the collision with a skill that came from years of piloting boats and a knowledge of the waterway.

"Fool tourists!" her father snapped, going back to his original course. "Get a man killed, they will."

Phoebe watched the sleek craft disappear

round another bend of the swamp and a bad feeling tingled inside her.

Her grandmother's house was built on a narrow spit of land that jutted out into the bayou. A plain, simple fisherman's house, her grandmother had added flowerbeds that were the envy of the community.

"Get the line, Phoebe," her father directed as he reversed the motor and slid the joe boat into the floating dock sideways. The boat slapped against the row of tyres that had been mounted there as a buffer. Her father was out of the boat in one lithe jump, carrying the shotgun easily.

Don't let it be a feud, Phoebe prayed as she wrapped the line round the mooring post. Despite their reluctant march into the twentieth century, many rural areas of Louisiana still maintained longstanding family fights that at times ended with someone getting hurt, sometimes even killed.

She hurried up the steps that, a few years back, her father and uncle had cut into the hillside and cemented to make a more gradual climb for Granmere to meet her

21

guests.

Her grandmother stood at the top of the hill. She wore one of her favourite flowered dresses and leant on a cane, her hair silvered and shiny. Phoebe went to her, arriving just after her father had given her a big hug.

Granmere Arceneaux was a big lady, with a lot of humour and genuine caring for others. "Oh, cher," she said. "You should see what them rascals has done to my garden."

"But you're all right?" her father asked as they followed the older woman round the house.

"Of course I'm all right. I called you, didn't I?"

"Them deputies, are they still here?"

"In back." Granmere waved to the rear of the house. "There's Marcel Landry's boy, TiBob, and a new man from New Orleans. Vern Haskell."

On the other side of the house, Phoebe saw the damage that had been done. *Oh no. Granmere must be heartbroken.*

The vandals had torn up most of the white picket fence that surrounded the herb garden.

Her grandmother had laboured in that half-acre plot for years to grow everything that she needed to take care of the sick in the community.

"This thing, you make someone mad?" Her father looked out over the garden with hard eyes.

"No," her grandmother said. "My herbs, my potions and medicines all work. No one say anything against me."

Phoebe looked at the pair of deputies at the side of the garden. Both of them wore crisp uniforms and ranger hats. TiBob Landry was her father's age, but the other deputy was younger. A moment later, they approached.

"Miz Joe," TiBob Landry said politely, touching his hat. Even though her grandfather had been dead ten years, everyone still addressed her grandmother by his name. "I'm afraid there's not much we can do here."

"Do you know who did it?" Phoebe's father asked.

Landry shook his head and looked

apologetic. "No, Cord, I don't. I thought maybe you could give me something to work with. A new feud, maybe?"

Her father shook his head. "No. And nobody would touch Mama. She doctors too many people in this here swamp. No one would want to destroy her garden like this. You want my money, I bet you it was someone from outside. Some of them oil trash brats in their fancy cars and big city ways."

"Come with me, cher," Granmere said, touching Phoebe's arm. "These men gonna be talking for a while yet, and it won't matter if we be there or not."

"I'm really sorry about the garden," Phoebe said as she let the older woman lead her away.

"It'll be hard, but I can rebuild," Granmere said. "That hurricane a couple years back, she tore up the garden something fierce."

"And totally flattened my school," Phoebe said. After the hurricane, DryadOil Corporation had offered to help the

24

community build a brand new high school. The oil workers and their families were thrilled. But many of the locals, like Phoebe's father, felt that it was just one more way for the oil company to take over the town.

Phoebe turned her gaze to the bayou and suddenly, without warning, the swirling, nauseous feeling returned. This time with more force. Phoebe bent over and tried to calm her stomach.

"Cher?" her grandmother said. "You all right?"

Phoebe tried to answer but couldn't. Voices assailed her. *Laughing. Taunting. Traces of fear mixed with anger and confusion. Shadows running, running, afraid of getting caught. "Old woman's a witch. Gonna put a hex on you."*

Her grandmother helped her to sit on the ground as the images retreated. "Are you OK?"

Phoebe looked at her grandmother, feeling cold inside. "The people who did this. They thought you were a witch. They destroyed your garden and they ran."

"You saw this?"

Phoebe nodded. "Just now."

"The *avartisment*, it was a very strong warning?"

"Yes." Phoebe tried to take slow, even breaths to get past the dizziness.

"Have you had them before?"

"This morning." Phoebe explained about Shiloh and the snake, and the vision that had followed almost immediately. "It was about this. It must have been at about the same time you called Papa."

"And now?" her grandmother prodded. "What did you see now?"

"Boys. But I couldn't make them out."

"What did you feel now?" Her grandmother's eyesight was limited these days but just now the woman's gaze was unwavering.

"Danger," Phoebe whispered.

"To yourself?"

"I don't know. And I don't want to know." Phoebe shook her head and squeezed her eyes shut, trying to rid her brain of any of the bad images.

"The time is coming soon, cher, and you will have to choose." Her grandmother gently touched her face and stroked her cheek. "Now, I go get you a tall glass of orange juice."

As her grandmother moved to the house, Phoebe stood up and turned her face into the wind. She breathed deep, smelling the scents carried on the breeze, listening to the distant caws of a crow. One of the drawbacks to being a Pisces was her highly developed sixth sense, which gave her the ability to see and hear things in other people's minds. She tried desperately to make the strange feeling of foreboding she'd received go away.

Instead, Phoebe sensed something magnetic calling out to her. She struggled to ignore it, walking away from the bayou with her eyes closed.

A few seconds later the sensation eased. She opened her eyes and found she was only a few steps from one of the sections of the picket fence still standing.

A flutter of yellow on the fence caught her

attention. At first she thought it was a flower, then realized it was too floppy. When she looked closer, she saw that it was a piece of material. Cotton. Maybe from a shirt or coat.

As she plucked it from the fence, a jolt of cold lightning zoomed through her fingertips, up her arm, and exploded in her brain. *Something bad is going to happen. Soon. Someone could even die.*

Phoebe gasped, staring at the piece of material in her hand.

"Cher?"

Phoebe whirled suddenly, as if caught doing something she shouldn't. Automatically she closed her fist over the material and tucked it into her jacket pocket. "Granmere, you startled me."

Her grandmother held out the glass of orange juice. "These *avartisments* take much from you, Phoebe." She stared at her. "You *will* tell me if you experience any more of them?"

"Of course," Phoebe lied. The image she had just received was too powerful and frightening to talk about. Phoebe finished her drink and handed the glass back to her grandmother. She felt refreshed but just as jittery.

Her father joined them and told her they had to go. They said their goodbyes, promising to return and help clean up the ravaged garden, and left. During the boat ride into Port Charmant, Phoebe was intensely aware of the torn material she'd tucked into her pocket. The sense of foreboding was muted, but still there. Something bad was definitely going to happen.

CHAPTER THREE

"*D*id you swim to school this morning, Phoebe?"

Ignoring Natalie Royster's comment, Phoebe handed her admit slip to Mr Burleson, the Louisiana History teacher that everyone thought was very cool because he listened to heavy metal music and encouraged his students to be creative.

With as much dignity as she could manage, Phoebe turned and looked for a desk. Seating wasn't assigned in Mr Burleson's room because he liked his students to be free to move about, sharing ideas and thoughts among themselves – as long as they did it in an orderly and productive fashion.

Three seats were empty. Two were near Natalie Royster and Missy Blume, leaders of the DryadOil Snobs, as Phoebe called them.

And one was beside Mark Chenier. Even though it was common knowledge that Mark was Natalie Royster's boyfriend, Phoebe couldn't stop her heart from racing a bit at the thought of sitting beside him. Mark saw her looking at him and responded with a friendly smile. A hot flush of embarrassment singed the back of Phoebe's neck and her cheeks.

"Phoebe," Mr Burleson said. "Is something wrong?"

"No." Despite her mud-splattered dress and wind-tangled hair, Phoebe made herself take the desk near Mark's. The chance to sit beside one of Port Charmant High's most popular and nicest guys didn't come along very often.

Mark had blond hair that was cut conservatively, a smooth face, and really dark blue eyes behind the lenses of his gold wire-framed glasses. He was wearing a dark oxford cloth shirt, tan chinos, and white Reebok high-tops. He sat up in his seat and nodded to Phoebe as she slipped into the desk next to him. Phoebe forced a stiff smile in reply.

"As I was saying..." Mr Burleson perched on the edge of the desk, his usual lecturing place when talking with the class. "I've been chosen to head this year's float presentation for the Port Charmant Mardi Gras. We've been given a generous endowment from DryadOil."

A small cheer went up in the corner of the room round Hunter Reed. Hunter clasped his hands, then shook them triumphantly, the way he did when he made a touchdown as the star fullback of the Port Charmant Princes. "That's my dad," he announced to the class. "I told him we could make a knockout float if we just had the dough. The company covered it."

Hunter was big and broad, with squared off fingers, white teeth and preppy clothes. His tan was a product of Christmas vacation spent in South America with his father, one of the top executives at DryadOil.

"It must be nice to have a father who's a vice president at a major oil company,"

Annalee Thibodeaux whispered from across the aisle. Annalee, like Phoebe, was one of the few Cajun students attending Port Charmant High.

Phoebe nodded her agreement, even as she thought to herself how she wouldn't have given her own father up for the world. A lot of the oilfield kids, Phoebe had noticed, talked down about their parents. Most of the Cajun kids didn't.

"Way to go, Hunter," K.J. Carmichael shouted, swapping high-fives with Hunter. K.J. was Hunter's sidekick and also the class clown, though most of the teachers didn't think him humourous at all. He was tall and thin, with a shock of red hair, freckles, and a big nose that his wit was sharp enough to work to his advantage rather than provide ammunition against him.

"It was nothing," Hunter said, leaning back. "Small change. My old man could've paid for it himself, but he knew the company could use the tax write-off."

"That boy, he got a mouth as big as a bullfrog," an angry voice muttered from the back corner of the class.

Phoebe didn't need to look to know the comment had come from her cousin TiChance. His real name was Lucien but everyone who knew him called him TiChance, which meant "little luck". The nickname had been given to him by Phoebe's grandfather. A few of the students had picked up on it, but most of the new teachers went by what was on his birth certificate.

TiChance was pure Aries, full of pride and energetic, but he carried an anger that Phoebe had never understood. He was as tall as Hunter, but leaner, and dark from the sun and weather instead of a trip to South America. His black hair was thick and shiny, and a lot of high school girls, Cajun as well as oilfield, talked about how they'd love to run their fingers through it.

TiChance wore faded jeans, a blue chambray work shirt with the sleeves cut out, and gleaming new cowboy boots with eagles stitched on the sides.

"Bullfrog?" Hunter clutched his heart, pretending to be wounded. "You really know how to hurt a guy."

The rest of class chuckled at Hunter, which only made TiChance more angry.

"If I could get your attention for just a moment," Mr Burleson said, taking a few steps into the aisle "I'd like to discuss what we're going to do for the float."

Phoebe bent down to place her books under her desk. Suddenly the sensation of dread capsized her hold on reality. The electricity jolted her out of her seat and she fell on her hands and knees, gasping.

"Phoebe!" Annalee cried. "Are you all right?"

Several in the classroom laughed. Phoebe could distinctly recognize Natalie's and Missy's voices.

She felt a warm hand on her arm. "Let me help."

It was Mark. He was kneeling next to her.

"Thanks," she croaked as he helped her stand. "I'm all right. Really."

Phoebe's knees felt a little wobbly but she wasn't about to admit that, not in front of this group.

"You dropped your book," Natalie announced, pointing at the comic book on the floor next to Phoebe's desk. Natalie twirled the end of her auburn ponytail round one finger as she waited for Phoebe's reaction.

"Extracurricular reading, Phoebe?" Missy Blume taunted. Missy's brown hair was cut short, emphasizing her high cheekbones and bringing out the amber-hazel eyes that she outlined with thick black liner. "I hope you had someone help you with the big words."

Phoebe stared down at the comic book next to her foot. There, for everyone to see, was *Commander Toad and the Planet of the Grapes*.

"It's my brother's," she said lamely, shoving it back in her schoolbag.

"Right." Missie rolled her eyes at Natalie.

"OK, people," Mr Burleson said. "Let's get back on track. There have been enough interruptions."

Phoebe sat down and stared hard at her hands clasped tightly on the desktop. She didn't think her face could get any warmer.

"This is only my second year here in Port Charmant," Mr Burleson said, "but I find myself fascinated with the culture all round us."

"Swamp hicks," K.J. muttered. "It *would* take a history teacher to be fascinated by swamp hicks."

"What I propose is that we make the float a historical tribute to the Cajun people," the history teacher went on. "Their heritage is unique, and this is a chance for those of us who are newcomers to learn about it. By the way, how many of you know where the Cajuns came from originally?" He looked round expectantly.

No one raised their hands. Especially not Phoebe, Annalee or TiChance.

"Come on," Mr Burleson said, with a smile. "Some of you are being shy. Annalee, why don't you tell us?"

"Canada," Annalee said quietly.

"Right. From Nova Scotia, on the Bay of Fundy."

He pulled down a map and extended his telescopic pointer to single out the area he was talking about. "They had come to the New World from France in the seventeenth century to escape religious persecution. They called their colony Acadia – that's Greek for 'land of milk and honey' – and soon were known as Acadians."

Please don't do this, Phoebe thought. *It's only going to make us stand out more, and we've all tried so hard to be like everyone else.* She glanced at Annalee and could tell that she was feeling the same. TiChance just looked angry.

"Many came as farmers and fur-trappers, indentured to the Company of New France."

"Them indentured people, they sound a lot like DryadOil employees if you ask me," TiChance said in a low voice.

"Hey, man," one of the oilfield kids named Keith said. "You take that back."

Hunter turned easily in his seat and locked eyes with TiChance. "Don't worry, Keith. TiChance didn't mean anything by that. Did you, TiChance?" He deliberately pronounced it the English way instead of the French *teeshawntz.*

38

TiChance looked away. "No. I didn't mean nothing."

"When the British took Nova Scotia from the French in 1755," the history teacher went on, "the Acadians were forced to leave. Louisiana was still French so they came here, and settled first in Bayou Teche, which includes our parish, Lafayette."

"They were given that land," TiChance pointed out, "because no one thought they could live on it."

Mr Burleson nodded. "It was not the most hospitable place to be."

"You'd think they would get the idea that they weren't wanted," Keith pointed out.

"But the Acadians – or Cajuns, as they'd come to be known – were very resourceful," Mr Burleson explained. "Each family was given an axe, a hoe, a scythe, a spade, two hens, a rooster, a two-month old pig and a ration of corn."

"And that's all they've got now," Keith added with a chuckle. "Not much ambition there."

TiChance was out of his chair in an

39

instant. He closed his hands into fists and there was murder in his eyes.

Phoebe leapt to her feet, blocking her cousin's path and locking eyes with him. "TiChance, please."

"Come on, swamp boy," Keith said, leaping out of his chair. "I'm ready for you."

TiChance put his hand on Phoebe's arm and started to shove past. But Hunter's voice stopped him. "TiChance, back off if you know what's good for you. And Keith, sit down and shut up."

Phoebe was really surprised when her cousin looked at Hunter, then did as the boy ordered. TiChance never backed away from a fight.

"Keith, TiChance," Mr Burleson said, "if there are any more problems in this class, both of you are going to owe me some time and some extra reports. I don't think either of you want that."

Both boys shook their heads and refused to look at each other.

"Anyway," Mr Burleson said, returning to the front of the class, "I'd like our float to reflect something of the Cajun history and culture." He leant on the edge of his desk. "Whereas other ethnic groups in the United States are struggling to hang on to their cultural identity, the Cajuns are flourishing. That's because they have a remarkably adaptable culture that's built for change. In everything they do – from food to architecture to social customs – they take in and absorb influences from the world round them. Yet the Cajuns remain very much themselves."

"Makes us sound really special," Phoebe whispered to Annalee.

"We may be special," Annalee rasped to Phoebe, "but once I leave this bayou, I ain't never coming back."

"Not even to see me?" Phoebe asked with more playfulness than she felt.

"I'll send you a bus ticket."

"It's that quality I'd like to capture for this year's float," Mr Burleson continued. "The way gumbo is made of a little bit of everything, with spices added to taste, creating something new each time. I want our float to stand out and say 'Cajun'."

He tried to give it the native inflection and Phoebe had to admit he came close.

"Annalee, Phoebe."

They looked at Mr Burleson.

"Do your parents have any pictures of past Mardi Gras celebrations here in Port Charmant?"

"Sure," Annalee said. "My dad even has some videotapes of a few of them."

Phoebe shrugged. "We have a few pictures, I suppose."

"Any costumes?" Mr Burleson asked. "I know a lot of people today dress as clowns, princes and your general Hallowe'en type monsters, but I would love to have some of the original beaded masks the women made, and any tapes of the music played back then."

"I can bring some masks," Annalee said quickly. "And my papa even has a Mardi Gras wagon we can use if I ask him. I know my mama has several masks and costumes we could alter to fit people or use as patterns for others."

"That's terrific. Just terrific." Mr Burleson was rubbing his hands together and beaming. "What about you, Phoebe?"

The only two truly Cajun girls in this class, and our families have to be feuding. Phoebe shook her head. "I don't think I can bring anything." She was suddenly conscious of every eye in the room on her.

"May I ask why?"

Phoebe took a deep breath. "Our families have a disagreement between us. If Annalee brought something, and I brought something, it would only make it worse." Her cheeks flamed.

"I'm afraid I don't understand." Mr Burleson arched one eyebrow.

"It would be like we were in competition," Phoebe explained. "My family's things against her family's things. This event would escalate and spill over out into the community. I've seen it happen before."

"You really think the actions of two high school girls showing bits and pieces of their cultural history could have that effect?"

"Yes." Phoebe knew it was true.

43

"Wow," Mark said. "I've heard about feuds in the history books, but I didn't know they were still going on."

Phoebe glanced at him and nodded.

"The feud was often a family's means of protecting its hunting and fishing rights," Mr Burleson said. "And could last for generations. How long has the one between the Thibodeauxs and the Arceneauxs been going on, Phoebe?"

She shrugged. "The families can't agree on that either."

"Sounds like something you'd see on a cartoon show with barefoot guys in overalls drinking moonshine and shooting at each other, to me," Missy said with a giggle.

The class exploded in laughter at Missy's description. Phoebe tried to ignore them by staring hard at one of the posters. The picture showed a tall cypress standing over a blue section of a wide bayou. Spanish moss was tangled in all the branches.

As she stared, Phoebe saw the water come to life, flowing across the poster. She felt the coolness sweeping in from the water.

Everyone else in the room melted from her sight as the bayou called out to her, then sucked her in. It felt like she was immersed in the water for a moment.

She leant back. When she did...

...it was night. She was afraid, lost, and someone was looking for her. She was near a bayou, but it wasn't the one in Mr Burleson's poster. This one was brown and sluggish, and mosquitoes buzzed round her head, choosing their spots. She was hiding behind a tree; the rough bark bit into her cheek while she leant against it, out of breath. Her heart pounded against her ribs.

Beams of light clawed through the tall trees round her. She could almost recognize where she was. Maybe she'd been through there at some time. Further on were headlights, still now, but the eddying dust in their glare showed the vehicle had been in motion until now.

"Over here!" someone whispered frantically. Men ran through the trees, and most of them had guns. Suddenly, one of them stepped into a clearing at her side. He was tall and broad

and looked Indian or Spanish, with short clipped hair but a long, flowing moustache. He started for her, pinning her with his flashlight.

"Run!" Phoebe yelled at herself. She stumbled, fell, and a flashlight beam passed over her as she rolled over and struggled to get to her feet. She pushed hard and a jolt of the now familiar electricity thrilled through her and—

—she screamed out loud, bringing her head up off her desk to look into the astonished eyes of the history class.

"Phoebe, you seem to be having a tough time today," Mr Burleson said, moving to her side.

Phoebe blinked at the students round her. That terrifying image had to have come from one of them. She shivered, suddenly icy cold. Someone was in trouble, whether they knew it or not, and the trouble would be coming soon. But who?

"Do you want to see the school nurse?" Mr Burleson asked.

"No," Phoebe murmured.

The vision was so compelling, that she couldn't keep her mind from it, replaying the images, shuffling them, trying to make sense of them. The men hadn't been hunting her. It was someone else. *And what were they going to do with that person when they found him or her?*

The bell rang abruptly and Mr Burleson shouted over the hubbub, "Listen, people, I want you to know you will be excused from your regular classes for the next two days as we attempt to put this float together to take part in the parade on Friday."

The announcement was met with an enthusiastic cheer. Getting out of class was a dream come true in the spring.

Phoebe, wanting to avoid any contact with the other students, spent a long time gathering her books and looping her purse over her shoulder. She was the last to leave the classroom and as she stepped through the door into the hall, she nearly crashed head-on into TiChance.

"Them people in that class," her cousin said in a raspy voice, "they got no business in

47

our business. You shouldn't be talking so much about our feuds and them things what belong to us alone. They're outsiders, Phoebe. They like it that way, and so do we." Without another word, he turned and was gone, presenting her with his broad, unforgiving back.

CHAPTER FOUR

"You should have seen yourself," Annalee chided after school that day. "You looked like you'd been possessed or something. I was expecting you to start spewing pea soup any time."

"Thanks a lot," Phoebe said. "Now I feel like a total idiot."

"Well, I thought you should know what you did. Kids talked about it all day."

"Oh, great!" Phoebe moaned, clutching her bookbag to her chest. The girls were on their way to the docks to be picked up by their fathers. The school buses didn't run that deeply into the bayou country. The dirt road leading to their home was a maze of ruts and big rocks, partially legitimized by the crushed clam shells poured over it, but too hard on an old bus.

"I was really embarrassed," Annalee continued.

This brought Phoebe up short. "Now why would you be embarrassed? I'm the one that fell out of my chair."

Annalee rolled her eyes. "Because whatever you do reflects on me. And anything I do reflects on you. That's just the way it is."

"Why should you care what people like Hunter Reed and Natalie Royster think? They're just a bunch of snots."

Annalee sighed. "Phoebe, take a look round. A good look." She waited a moment while Phoebe did that, then kicked a clam shell across the rutted road. "This is Port Charmant, home of crawfish and craw-fishermen. If we're not careful, we're going to end up just like this road. It looks like it's going somewhere, but where does it go?"

Phoebe didn't answer.

"I'll tell you where," Annalee said. "Right into the swamp – and it never comes out again. Phoebe, this is our last year of school. Our last chance to find a way out of the bayous. Do you have a scholarship to college?"

"No. Not yet."

"Neither do I. And if we don't go to college, then we're going to have to try to get a job, with luck at DryadOil. But we'll never get hired by that company if you go round acting like you're possessed."

"Well, I'm sorry to embarrass you," Phoebe snapped. "But it wasn't my fault. I was looking at that poster of the swamp and suddenly I was hit with this overpowering vision—"

Annalee waved her hand to stop Phoebe. At the same time she looked over her shoulder to make sure no one was listening. "Lower your voice, will you? And quit talking about visions."

"That's what it was, Annalee," Phoebe said quietly. "And if you don't like it, I can't do anything about that. But what I saw was very scary. I don't know who it was about, but I think we all need to watch our steps."

Annalee stared at Phoebe and shivered. "You're giving me the creeps."

"I can't help it." Phoebe replied. "I'm a Pisces and an Arceneaux. Granmere says that's a powerful combination, and the reason I have the gift."

"I swear," Annalee said, "sometimes I get the impression that you'd be happy to spend the rest of your life here as a swamp girl."

"If that was true, I wouldn't even be talking to you," Phoebe said. "Your family and mine are sworn enemies."

"I'm only distantly related to those Thibodeauxs. I shouldn't even be part of that feud."

"It's in the blood," Phoebe said. "You can't escape it. Even if only one drop of the blood in your veins is Thibodeaux, that makes you a Thibodeaux."

"God, but you can be so old-fashioned."

"I can't help it. It's not my choice to carry on the traditions. They just keep getting handed to me."

As the girls walked towards the docks, Phoebe noticed the gleaming roofs of new office buildings that had begun to spring up along Main Street. Many smaller businesses had been relocated to make room for DryadOil's corporate branch headquarters, and others had been forced to close their doors for ever when the oil company opened their own supply stations.

"So what started the feud, anyway?" Annalee asked.

"I think it was about territorial rights," Phoebe replied. An orange-and-blue helicopter roared by overhead, streaking for the helipad that had been chopped out of the swamp less than a mile from town. "A Thibodeaux was hunting on land claimed by the Arceneaux."

Shading her eyes, Phoebe saw that it was one of the big helicopters that ferried the drilling crews back and forth to the offshore drilling rigs out in the Gulf. Its pontoons looked enormous.

"When?"

Phoebe looked back at her friend. "When what?"

"When did this trespassing thing happen?" Annalee asked.

"About a hundred and fifty, hundred and seventy years ago."

"You've got to be kidding!" Annalee puffed out her cheeks in frustration. "That's ancient history! Why does the feud between the families keep going on?"

Phoebe shrugged. "A feud brings up lots of emotions on both sides. Nobody wants to admit they're wrong, so both sides don't talk. Pretty soon something else happens, gets it all stirred up again. Like now."

"What's going on now?"

"You know those old hunting trailers down on the south edge of Richelieu Bayou?" Phoebe asked.

"Not exactly," Annalee replied. "Most of the families have camps down on Richelieu."

"Well, that campsite, it's always been for the bayou families. Everyone knows that. But now your cousin Didier Thibodeaux is leasing his trailers out to tourists who want to go fishing and hunting."

"Phoebe, those trailers are nothing but tin bug-traps. I think Didier's got sense. When they're not being used by the families, those trailers can make them money."

"That's not the way it sits with my

family," Phoebe sighed. "Papa says those campsites are the last place we haven't let the oilmen into. They're already trampling all over the place like an invading army, with their fast boats and Jeeps and guns. The bayous feed lots of people round here. Why trash them any more than necessary?"

They had reached the dock and Annalee looked out over the water. "My daddy's not here yet. And neither is yours."

Nearly two dozen small boats were tied up round the dock, where fishermen were talking with each other about their day or mending their nets or helping someone else mend theirs.

"Annalee?" Phoebe murmured. "Were all the kids really talking about me?"

"Not all," Annalee conceded. "Just a few. And if it's any consolation, Natalie was really angry with Mark for all the attention he paid you. By sixth period she was snapping at him like an old mud turtle."

Phoebe grinned at the thought. "I'd love to see Natalie covered in mud. She really is the most stuck-up girl at school. How Mark could even talk to her is beyond me."

"She may be stuck-up, but that's because she's beautiful and rich," Annalee said, picking up a pebble and tossing it at the water.

"That's true," Phoebe admitted with a shrug of one shoulder.

"And when she wants to, Natalie can be pretty funny," Annalee said. "I've heard her tell jokes on the quad at lunchtime and everybody laughs."

"Making fun of people less fortunate than yourself is not my idea of a joke," Phoebe muttered, as she sat down on the edge of the pier and dangled her legs over the side. "I've heard her do that more than once."

Annalee plopped down beside Phoebe. "She does have a mean streak. There's no denying that."

"Maybe Mark's as mean as she is, and I just haven't seen it."

Annalee shook her head. "No, that boy is for real. He says hello to everyone in the halls, but not in a loud way, like Hunter or K.J. He seems, I don't know...gentle."

Phoebe smiled wistfully. "Mark's an Aquarius, which means he has a good heart and deals with people fairly and squarely. I guess that's why he holds so many offices at school."

"It doesn't hurt that he's got a French last name," Annalee pointed out. "Even the Cajuns trust him."

"Yeah," Phoebe sighed. "And he's so good-looking."

"Phoebe, I don't need the gift to tell you're working on a major heartbreak with Mark," Annalee said, waggling her finger at Phoebe. "Does the name Natalie Royster mean anything to you? Take my advice and put him out of your head."

"I can't," Phoebe confessed. Her thoughts were constantly filled with images of him. Mark smiling at her in class. Mark nodding hello in the halls. She'd even secretly written his name paired with hers in her diary.

"Oops," Annalee squeaked, suddenly leaping to her feet. "Your daddy's here."

Phoebe looked out at the bayou and saw her father pulling up to the dock and hopped to her feet, too. "I'd better run."

"Remember, you haven't been talking to me, you don't know me, and you're waiting till I die so you can celebrate the conquest of yet another Thibodeaux."

"Right." Phoebe heaved her schoolbag on to her shoulder.

"And tomorrow," Annalee admonished, "no fainting spells, no swamp visions."

Phoebe said goodbye and hurried to meet her father.

He regarded her suspiciously. "You been talking to that Thibodeaux girl?"

"Homework, Papa," she said, shoving her schoolbag under the bench in the boat. "I was late this morning and missed English Lit., remember?"

He nodded and powered the joe boat out into the bayou. As they bounced along on top of swirling brown ripples, Phoebe made a conscious effort not to look in the water. She could still feel the electricity buzzing round inside her stomach and she was afraid of what terrible vision she might find beneath the surface.

CHAPTER FIVE

That evening, while her grandmother talked to the social worker who visited once a month about her fading eyesight, Phoebe worked in the small, immaculate kitchen sorting through the herbs that had been salvaged from the garden. She separated them, then put them into plastic bags to be processed in the next few days.

A flock of orange and yellow running lights whisked by on the bayou. Warned by the thrum of powerful motors, she looked up in time to see the black Cris-Craft go speeding by. Then it was gone.

Phoebe ran out the back door to catch another glimpse of it, but she was too late.

"Is something wrong, cher?"

She turned and saw her grandmother making her way towards her. The social worker was getting in her car and leaving. "A boat just went by. One I don't know."

"Them boats, there be plenty of them in the bayous now that them oil company fellas move into Port Charmant. Always going. Up the bayou, down the bayou. Never go slow, always fast."

"I know." She shrugged it off.

"What about the *avartisment*, cher? Have you seen anything?"

At first Phoebe wanted to say no. But looking round the bayou surrounding her, she decided to tell her grandmother what had happened at school that morning.

Her grandmother listened and then took her hand. "Your powers are going to be very strong, cher. Very strong. You've been truly blessed with the gift."

"Gift?" Phoebe echoed. "It's more like a curse. I feel so...so out of control when I'm having one of those things."

Her grandmother led her to two folding chairs by the ruined fence. "Cher, people are given a power for a reason. My hands, they were strong and fine in their time, able to raise the healthy plants and minister to the sick. I brought babies into this world, and I buried them as men and women. It's time I stopped and let someone else be Port Charmant's healer, their *traiteur*."

"Granmere, you still have a lot of years left." It distressed Phoebe to hear her grandmother talk like that.

Her grandmother chuckled. "Silly girl, I'm not talking about dying. There just needs to be a younger woman to take care of the community. Someone who travels more easily than I do. I'd like for that to be you."

"I'm seventeen. I'm not ready for that."

"Ah, cher, I was but fifteen when my granmere passed me the herbs and the secrets and had me start taking care of people."

Phoebe could feel her chest constrict at the thought of being trapped in a life in the swamps. "But there's so many things that I want to do. I don't want to stay here for ever."

Her grandmother reached out and covered Phoebe's face with a callused palm. "There's a boy. Someone special. But he's not Cajun."

"Granmere, please."

The old woman laughed quietly. Behind her, the moon lay on the horizon, a ghost of itself in the dark clouds. She took her hand away. "Have you told him you like him?"

"No."

"Why?"

"Because he's got a girlfriend."

"I've found in my years of doctoring," her grandmother said, "that girlfriends are not always a serious condition. Sometimes they go away all by themselves."

"I wish," Phoebe said, with a chuckle.

"But we must talk of the gift," her grandmother said, taking both of Phoebe's hands in hers. "You've been given a powerful warning, cher. It's not wise to ignore such things."

Phoebe felt frustrated. One second Annalee was pulling her out of the swamp, and the next her grandmother was pushing her further and further in. "All I want to know is what to do."

Luckily, her grandmother thought she was talking about the visions. "You pay attention to them dreams, cher, and it will all be made clear to you. But you must listen."

"All my life you've been telling me to listen and use the gift," Phoebe said.

"But not until this morning did you know its strength," her grandmother reminded her. "This morning, when you come upon little Shiloh laying on the ground like that with Mr Cottonmouth looking to maybe bite him on the nose, you called up the power. Now, it's like a door, you done flung it open and you ain't gonna get it closed again."

I don't know if I want it open, Phoebe thought, with a shiver.

Her grandmother fumbled in the pocket of her dress and brought out a torn and twisted plant. "Do you know what this is?"

Phoebe took the plant and looked at it. In the fading light it looked much darker than it would normally. It had egg-shaped leaves with opposing leaf placement and small, bluish-purple flowers. "Easy," she said confidently. "This is woody nightshade."

"Yes. And it can be used to make the rheumatism medicine."

"If you can find it," Phoebe said, turning the plant over. "It's kind of early in the year for nightshade."

"Yes but I was growing some in the garden greenhouse. Now it's all gone, but Tante Tina, she still needs some to relax her old bones. I don't want to let her down. I want you to find some for me."

"How?"

"I show you." Her grandmother folded the plant into Phoebe's palm, then made a fist round it. "Feel the plant, cher. Close your eyes and look for it. Don't feel for them plants that's too young. Feel for the older ones. They're out there, hard to find, sure, but out there all the same."

The cold electricity in Phoebe's stomach sparked and filled her like a cold wave. She felt herself move forward, then take a step...

...and she was looking at a stand of woody nightshade along the bayou bank under an overhang of thick cypress. Only a few of the plants were in early bloom, but she knew they would be enough to serve Granmere's purposes. She turned round and round, but

64

she couldn't find her grandmother. Only the bayou stretched in both directions. Dark had gathered, pooling shadows on the water beneath the cypress trees.

"Granmere?"

"Shush, cher. I am with you. No reason to be afraid. Do you know where you are?"

"Further north on Blackcat Bayou. Maybe two miles from my home. Near Teche's Finger."

"Yes, I've found nightshade there before. And there is some flowering?"

Phoebe didn't nod because she didn't know if her grandmother could see her. "Yes."

"You can find your way there?"

"Yes."

"Then come back to me."

Phoebe felt her grandmother's hand on hers, and stepped back—

—into the ravaged garden. Phoebe blinked. It seemed so real.

"The power is very strong in you, cher," Granmere said. "I went there with you, and I did not mean to."

"You felt it?"

"The electricity. Yes, I felt it. The power takes different forms in different people. My own, it pulls at me like saltwater taffy straight from the cookpot." The old woman pushed herself up and started back to the house. "Come, there is a recipe I need you to take to Tante Tina on your way home. Tomorrow, I'd like for you to go to Teche's Finger and gather up as much of the nightshade as you can find. My medicines are understocked now, and there may be much sickness with all the spring rains a-coming."

Phoebe pressed a hand to her stomach, amazed at what had just happened to her. She had somehow left her body and travelled to another part of the swamp and yet her grandmother acted as if it was an everyday occurrence.

"I pay you for your time after school tomorrow, cher," Granmere said.

"No, I couldn't take any money from you."

"Then, cher, if my money's no good with

66

you, maybe I whip you up a nice love potion, eh?"

Phoebe's eyes widened. Love potions definitely fell into the "witch" territory, a place Phoebe wanted to stay far away from.

Phoebe was relieved when her grandmother laughed. "I'm only joking, cher. You got yourself and that's all the potion you need."

Her grandmother handed her a sheet of writing paper that bore a curious shorthand that so many of the other old ladies seemed to understand, and kissed Phoebe on the cheek. "I'll see you tomorrow then."

Phoebe nodded. "Tomorrow." She hurried down to the *pirogue,* anxious to get going before it got too dark.

Tante Tina lived on the bayou in a trailer house less than a mile from Phoebe's grandmother. Twenty years before, the trailer had been shiny and new. Now the swamp had claimed it, with mossy fingers gripping the sides and tree branches thrusting out over its roof.

Tante Tina was waiting on the boat dock

when she arrived.

"Your granmere called me on the telephone, cher," the gnarled old woman said. "Let me know you was coming. Just hand that recipe up here and you best be getting on home. Your mama, she's gonna be worried some."

"Yes, ma'am." Phoebe passed the letter up, noticing how jerky Tante Tina's movements were. She knew her rheumatism must be flaring up something awful. "I'm getting that nightshade tomorrow, and Granmere will have your medicine to you soon."

"Thank you, cher. You don't know what a godsend your granmere is to an old woman like me."

Watching Tante Tina hobble up the steps, Phoebe decided not to wait until tomorrow. *She's in so much pain. I can go tonight. Papa will understand.*

She looked round at the darkness that had filled the spaces between the bayou water and the trees and hung a running light on the prow of the *pirogue* so other boats could see her coming.

Out in the middle of the sluggish water, but moving along at a good speed, Phoebe let her tired arms rest for a few moments. Swamp gas, backlit by the moon till it burned harsh and greyish-white, drifted through the trees and brush like searching ghosts.

She put her hands in the pockets of her sweater and felt the tingle of electricity. Drawing it out, she looked at piece of material she'd found on her grandmother's fence that morning.

She closed her hand round it, then shut her eyes, looking inwards the way her grandmother had coached her to do. The electricity spread. An image formed inside her head. She could hear voices – boys, laughing, whispering, on the edge of frantic, as they ripped through the white picket fence...

"Hurry," somebody urged, *"we don't want that old bag to catch us."*

"Why? You afraid she's going to turn you into a toad or something?" The other boy laughed.

Phoebe looked round at the shadows moving across the garden, but the moonlight was weak and her eyes didn't exactly do what she wanted them to. It took her a minute to realize that she was seeing through someone else's eyes. Someone who'd been there. Someone who'd helped destroy Granmere's garden.

Angry, she tried to move her head and see the people ripping up plants in front of her. But she couldn't. She was suddenly aware of the rough wood in her hand. Then she was pulling, pulling hard. There was a sick feeling in her stomach, but she didn't know if it was from her or from the person she was feeling the experience through.

"Think the sheriff'll come looking for us at school tomorrow?" someone asked.

"You worry too much. Keep pulling."

"Hey," another voice said, "somebody just turned a light on."

Phoebe's view suddenly switched to Granmere's house, and sure enough a light was on. But she knew that Granmere got up several times during the night. Her *grandmother hadn't known her garden was being destroyed then.*

However, it scared the boys responsible for the destruction. They fled the garden. Whoever she was remembering through turned and ran, jumping over a section of the fence still standing. When the shirt caught on the fence, it made the runner stagger, causing a fall that—

—jarred Phoebe in the *pirogue*. Dazed from the vision and its clarity, she unconsciously grabbed the sides of the boat and stared wildly into the water to see what she'd hit.

There, just cruising away towards the bank, were the cold reptilian eyes of a full-grown 'gator that had nearly overturned the *pirogue* in the middle of the bayou.

Phoebe's heart raced when she thought about what had almost happened. *Calm down, just breathe again.* She did. Then she picked up the oars and rowed away from the area towards Teche's Finger. The farther she got from the 'gator, the more angry she became about the vision.

Phoebe was convinced that if she'd been

able to see the boys responsible for tearing up Granmere's garden that she'd have known who they were. She was certain she went to school with them.

CHAPTER SIX

Phoebe's flashlight beam fell across a raccoon husking out a stubborn clam at the edge of Blackcat Bayou. Its eyes turned firefly green for an instant, then it cleared the area in one lithe jump.

Teche's Finger was a narrow spit of land that disappeared every time the water level of the bayou rose during the spring and autumn. Hardly anything grew there, but it was a haven for nightcrawlers and salamanders and most of the local fishermen knew that. Phoebe had gathered them herself.

Phoebe, clutching a burlap bag in one hand and her flashlight in the other, was trudging through the broken limbs and blackberry brambles in search of the nightshade for Tante Tina. She was cold and anxious to get home.

Behind her, the low rumble of a powerboat echoed along the bayou.

Phoebe froze where she stood, isolating the sound from the burping bullfrogs, cries of nightbirds, and insistent high-pitched buzzes of mosquitoes. It was coming from upstream.

More cautious than afraid, Phoebe closed the bag she was using to collect the nightshade and stepped back into the shadowy shelter of the thick cypress near Teche's Finger. She turned off the flashlight.

The powerboat pulled in to the opposite bank and stopped. Uncertain moonlight spilled on to the boat and its passenger, though she felt certain she'd have recognized TiChance even under more difficult circumstances. She started to yell a hello, but then remembered how he'd been that morning in class. She kept quiet.

A lantern flickered at the top of the hill facing Teche's Finger, then swept round and pointed at TiChance. It also revealed two men dressed in dark clothing and a white van sitting silently beside them.

"What you boys waiting on?" TiChance

asked, standing at the bottom of the tree-lined incline and looking up.

"Somebody was out there," one of the men replied. "Saw a light a minute ago."

Oh god. Phoebe drew further back into the tree. She didn't want them to find her. Everything in her said these men were bad. The electricity in her stomach coiled restlessly, getting stronger. *TiChance, what have you gotten yourself into?*

"Probably just a hunter," her cousin said. "I don't see no light now. You boys ready to go or not?"

"Don't get mouthy, kid."

"You know another guide can get you through this bayou, fetch him up," TiChance shot back.

The two men descended with the lantern swinging wildly in front of them. Phoebe strained to see their faces but the gloom was too deep. Then, when the guy with the lantern was clambering aboard TiChance's powerboat, the light fell over the hard planes of the man's face. He had a moustache—

—and he was pointing right at her,

shouting, "There he is! Come on!" He sprinted at her, using the flashlight in his hand to knock aside the branches and brush.

Phoebe ran, but she knew she was using someone else's legs, felt someone else's heart slamming inside his ribs. Teche's Finger had disappeared. So had the bayou. She ran away from the men into the unfamiliar forest ahead of her. Branches slapped at her, hit her in the face. She felt the pain, but it was borrowed, once removed.

"Don't let him get away!" another man yelled. "He saw us and can identify us. If you have to, kill him!"

Knowing she was trapped in the same vision she'd had at school didn't help. Phoebe wanted to scream. Instead, she ran. The feet she was using sank into the loamy ground. She grabbed a tree and used it to change direction, hanging on. The bark shredded the skin on her palm and wrist and she felt blood start to well up.

Without warning she ran into a dead end. Walled on three sides by the ravine she hadn't seen until it was too late, she turned round.

The man with the flashlight was on her, grabbing her jacket with one hand. "I got him!" the man yelled. "I got him!"

Phoebe tried to get away, tried to kick the man.

"Stupid move, kid. This didn't have to be done the hard way." The moustached man swung the heavy flashlight. It connected solidly with Phoebe's head and she felt herself sinking, drowning in the whirling night then—

—she gazed up at the night sky. The stars were diamond bright and she knew she wasn't where she had been only a moment ago. She sat up cautiously, listening for voices, for the powerboat. But heard nothing of them. She couldn't remember falling. When she looked, Teche's Finger and the bayou were where they were supposed to be but the powerboat and TiChance and the men were gone. However, the four-wheel drive van was still parked on the hilltop.

C'mon, Phoebe. Now's your chance. Get your feet moving and get out of here. She stood despite the spinning sensation in her head. She picked up the burlap bag of nightshade and quietly made her way to the *pirogue*. She didn't wear a watch so she didn't know how long the vision had taken. She climbed inside the boat and poled off, then used the oars.

The visions meant something. She knew that. But were they of things to come? Or were they things that had already happened? When she touched the scrap of cloth that she'd found on her grandmother's fence, she knew she was remembering events that had already transpired.

What did these other visions mean? Who was being chased? And why? And who were the men with TiChance and what were they doing in the bayou?

They hadn't moved like someone used to the swamp. She kept the oars moving, not really knowing what to do.

What if her vision was of TiChance? What if he never came out of the swamp again? Would it be her fault for not paying closer attention to her visions?

CHAPTER SEVEN

*Appearances can be deceiving. A Pisces
usually isn't fooled by outward shows but
the planets are playing tricks up there, and
the Moon is about to pull your tides into an
emotional quagmire. Don't let your heart
rule your head. Think it through first.*

"Hello, Phoebe."

Phoebe looked up from the strip of muslin
she was working on and nearly knocked over
her bucket of water. "Mark!"

He stood in the middle of the auto body
shop, where Mr Burleson's class was
working on the float, clutching a half-dozen
dead cypress roots. "I've been meaning to
ask you how you're feeling today."

"Fine." Phoebe forced herself to act

casual. She dipped some more muslin in her bucket and laid it across the chicken wire mould that had been shaped to look like a riverbank. "I guess it was some kind of twenty-four-hour flu bug."

"It really hit you hard," Mark replied.

Phoebe felt her cheeks heat up at the memory of falling to her knees in front of the entire history class. "That was pretty embarrassing," she said, suddenly aware of what she might look like. Her overalls were covered in plaster and strands of her blonde hair, which she'd pulled into a plait under her bandanna, were dangling in her face. She knew they must be crusted with plaster. She shook them away, adding, "But thanks for helping me."

"It was my pleasure." Mark smiled as if he meant that.

Phoebe wiped her face with the back of her hand, hoping she wasn't smearing plaster on her nose. "What are you doing with those roots?"

Mark looked at them as if trying to figure that out. Then it clicked. "Mr Burleson said we might want to use them on the pieces you're working with. Once we get the riverbank painted and built, it'll look more authentic if it has roots wrapped round it, too."

Phoebe nodded. "That's a good idea. Why don't we position them and see what we're working with?"

Working carefully, aware of the wet plaster, they looped the branches over the muslin and chicken wire. Phoebe soon got caught up in the arranging and started talking more. The ideas flowed so quickly between them that it was amazing. She couldn't believe they talked so easily.

Mr Burleson's idea had been to build a section of bayou on the flatbed trailer float and depict all the cultural influences on Cajun history. Using the river (made of sheets of wrinkled aluminum foil painted a light blue with white-capped detailing) as a time line, the float would display bayou life from the first Acadians through to the present-day Cajuns.

"I think that'll do it," Mark said as he

looked at the arrangement Phoebe had suggested.

"We can weave those roots the length of the float," Phoebe said.

"I like it," Mark said. "Subtle, but it carries impact."

Phoebe nodded, very pleased with herself. "If we sketch a diagram of the configuration, then number the roots you're holding, we should be able to put them back when the painting is finished."

"Great idea." Mark took a pencil from his pocket. "I'll mark the roots."

Phoebe started sketching.

"Hey, you're not bad," Mark said, peering over her shoulder.

"Only when I'm sketching the bayou," Phoebe replied. "I could draw it with my eyes closed. But thanks, I love to draw."

"I like working with my hands, too," Mark said. "That's why Mr Burleson put me on this part of the float. He's seen some of the models I've done."

"What kind of models do you make?"

Mark shrugged. "Ships. I like the old ones

best, British frigates, Phoenician merchants, Roman galleys. Anything that's sail-driven. I know some other guys who are into modelling, but they work from kits."

"If you don't have a kit, how do you build them?" Phoebe asked.

Mark looked uncomfortable. "You sure you really want to hear this? I didn't mean to talk about it so much."

"I think it's interesting." Across the shop floor, Phoebe saw Annalee looking at her, then give her a thumbs up when no one was watching. Phoebe responded with a very pleased half-smile.

"First I get as many different pictures of a ship I want to build as I can," Mark said as he helped her dip and drape the muslin. "Front, sides, top, and bottom view. Then I sketch it out, getting it totally into my mind, and I break it down into sections. Once I get the sections, I can figure out what kind of wood I need and how I need to shape it. I carve and sand most of it, then glue it together. It takes a lot of time."

Phoebe liked hearing this. A lot. "So what

got you interested in ships?" she asked, wiping the plaster on the leg of her overalls, not caring any more what she looked like. They were working.

Mark grinned. "You're going to think this is dumb."

Phoebe put her hands on her hips. "No, I won't. Try me."

"Promise not to tell?"

"Cross my heart," Phoebe said, making a little plaster "x" on the bib of her overalls.

"When I was a kid," Mark whispered conspiratorially, "I wanted to be a pirate when I grew up."

"Not you!" Phoebe gave him a look of mock astonishment.

He nodded enthusiastically. "That's why I love it that we live here. I heard that pirates used to lurk in these waters."

Phoebe nodded. "Jean Lafitte was our most famous pirate. His ghost pops up everywhere. And there's the Pirate Ghost of Gombi Island. He's very famous."

Mark grinned crookedly at her. "Maybe someday we can go on a ghost hunt. In search of pirates."

Phoebe wiped her hands. "I'd like that."

Natalie Royster suddenly stuck her face between them and glared at Phoebe. "I certainly hope I'm not intruding here."

Returning Natalie's gaze, Phoebe said, "No."

"You two looked entirely too cosy over here alone." Natalie smiled at Mark. "I thought I'd better break things up."

Mark wiped his hands on the corner of his work shirt. "We were just talking, getting the float together."

Natalie turned her back on Phoebe, acting as if she wasn't even there. "I wanted to talk to you this morning, Mark, but you got to school late. I tried calling you last night. Your mother said you weren't home."

"I wasn't. I was out getting some wood for the new model I'm building. I told you I was going to do that."

"You were supposed to meet us downtown. We went to the movies without you."

"I never agreed to that, Natalie. You said

you were going with your friends."

"Well, your attendance is required tonight," Missy Blume said, joining them. "We're all going out to teach Natalie how to fish. It's Hunter's idea. We'll have a picnic outdoors, and a bonfire along the river. It'll be a blast." She looked at Natalie and Mark. "You two lovebirds don't want to spoil it by fighting, do you?"

Both of them shook their heads.

"Natalie! Missy!" K.J. yelled from across the auto body shop. "We need some help here. Hunter's getting ready to do some hammering and I'm not about to hold the nails."

As Natalie turned to leave, she called over her shoulder, "Well, I'm glad somebody needs me."

Mark winced. "Natalie can get pretty jealous," he explained with an embarrassed shrug.

Phoebe nodded. "I can see that."

"Anyway..." Mark cleared his throat awkwardly and changed the subject. "Have you ever been to that little grocery store down by the dock?"

"The White Stag Mercantile?" Phoebe asked. "Sure."

Mark nodded. "Have you ever seen that boat over the counter? The one in the glass bottle?"

"Yes. My uncle made it for Mr Rigaud thirty years ago when he opened the store."

"You're kidding." Mark's eyes shone brightly. "All the books I've been able to get my hands on, none of them have ever showed how to do that."

"I'm sure my uncle could show you how. He's a fisherman and usually after school he's down at the docks." She looked at him and was afraid when she considered her next words. "If you'd like, I could introduce you some time."

"I'd like that. How about this afternoon?" He hesitated. "I mean, if it's not a problem."

Phoebe, scarcely able to contain her excitement, tried to keep her voice steady. "That's fine with me, but I thought you had a fishing party to go to."

"It can wait awhile. They won't be getting

together until about seven or so."

"All right, people, it's time to start cleaning up," Mr Burleson announced from the centre of the room. He was in work clothes with paint smears all over his shirt and face. His group had been painting the structures that would sit on top of the float. "Good work today."

Phoebe put the muslin and spatulas away while Mark went to empty the coffee cans filled with water. As soon as he'd gone, Annalee hurried over, smiling in an I-told-you-so way. "Well?"

"We're going to the Mercantile after school to look at Mr Rigaud's ship in a bottle," Phoebe whispered.

"Want some company?" Annalee teased.

"No way."

Annalee laughed. "Mark is very interested in you."

"How can you tell? You weren't even here."

"Body language," Annalee said. "I could tell by the way he was moving round you."

Phoebe was determined not to get her

hopes up, in spite of the fact that Natalie and Mark seemed not to be getting along. "I think you were just seeing things."

Annalee put one hand on Phoebe's shoulder. "My papa is one of the best traders on the bayou. No one gets the best of him. He's taught me how to look at a person and know if the time you invest in them is going to be worth your while. I think your time is well spent." Annalee wiggled her eyebrows. "Let me know if I'm wrong."

Phoebe chuckled and then hurried to the lab sinks at the back of the warehouse. She turned on both taps in the industrial sized sink.

"I'm ready when you are," Mark said, joining her. He had removed his work shirt and put on his coat.

"I'm just about finished," Phoebe said, turning to look back at the sink that was filling with water. The swirl of water and paint sent a blast of cold electricity into her brain.

"*...the witch's house,*" someone said. "*Are you afraid she's going to turn you into* *a toad?"*

Her hand, the one that had belonged to someone else two nights ago, was tight on the fence.

"Let's kick this fence down too," someone else said. "We can be out before she—"

"Phoebe, are you OK?" Mark touched her arm. She was clutching the side of the sink, trying hard to stay on her feet.

Phoebe turned to face him, trying to make herself say yes, when she noticed the hole in the lining of Mark's jacket. The fabric inside the denim material was yellow flannel, the same colour as the piece of material she'd found on her grandmother's fence. "You were there," she said in a hollow voice.

"What?"

A leaf clung to the underside of his jacket sleeve and she plucked it off. "This is woody nightshade. It was supposed to be medicine for Tante Tina, but you and your friends destroyed my grandmother's garden." She was shaking as she faced him. Her anger and hurt and confusion grew.

"Phoebe, wait a minute!" Mark released

her arm and took a step back.

"No! You were there, Mark!"

Pain showed in his eyes.

"You helped destroy my grandmother's garden. You called her a witch."

Mark stepped back until he was pressed up against the lab sink. He held his hands in front of him as if he was afraid of getting hit.

Phoebe wanted to strike out, but didn't. "You were there. And this proves it." She pulled the piece of material from her purse and threw it at him. It fluttered and landed on the ground between them.

Other kids were watching now, and Mr Burleson was making his way towards them.

"I thought you were different from these other oil field trash," Phoebe said. "I thought you were a good person. I was stupid. You're just like all the others."

"Phoebe," Mark croaked.

But she couldn't listen to him. Her eyes were filling with tears, for herself, for her grandmother, and for Mark, though he didn't deserve them. She turned and fled from the shop. "Stay away from me!"

Outside, the moist air told her it was going to rain soon. She hoped it would come down long enough and hard enough to spoil Mark's fishing trip with Natalie and all the rest of them.

"Phoebe, please!" Mark caught up with her, grabbing her arm.

She spun angrily. "What can you possibly tell me that's going to make me feel any different than I do right now?"

"I didn't know it was your grandmother's house—" Mark stopped speaking abruptly and his face went ashen. He slipped back inside the shop doors, his eyes on the gravelled road.

Her attention drawn, Phoebe glanced out at the road and saw a late model white van cruise slowly by. The brake lights flared for just an instant as it slowed to stop, then it continued on.

When she looked back at the shop doors Mark was gone. Choking back a sob, Phoebe headed for the main school building to get her books. She felt like a fool for ever believing in him. But there was no

way she was ever going to make that
mistake again.

93

CHAPTER EIGHT

"Help!"

The voice held such a note of sheer terror that Phoebe sat up at once and looked round for the screamer.

Only her empty bedroom greeted her. *It was just a dream.* She sighed in relief and hugged herself reassuringly. The room was in total darkness except for the narrow bands of moonlight creeping in through the blinds over her window. The alarm clock showed eleven o'clock.

Knowing she wouldn't be able to get back to sleep right away, Phoebe shoved the blankets aside and got out of bed. The night's chill flowed round her as she pulled on her robe and stuck her feet into her slippers.

Whose voice was that? she thought, as she looked out the window over the bayou woods. An owl took flight and glided across the indigo skyline just above the trees. *I'm certain I know.* She was convinced that it belonged to a boy. *TiChance? Has he got into trouble with those two men he met last night?* She hadn't mentioned the incident to her father and now she wished she had.

Off in the distance, through the breath-fogged window, Phoebe thought she saw pinpricks of light. *Torches? Lanterns?* She wasn't sure, but the only thing off in that direction were a few tumbledown fishing and hunting shacks. The lights were gone when she blinked.

Phoebe hadn't told her father about finding out that Mark had helped destroy Granmere's garden either. It was easy to talk to her parents most of the time, but now she was holding on to these secrets. She didn't like it, but didn't know what else to do.

Just as her mind started to rehash the fight she'd had with Mark, the phone rang.

Who would be calling at this hour? She hurried to the phone in the kitchen. "Hello?"

"Phoebe?" a man's voice said. "This be

Achilles Pailet, from down at the dock."

"Yes, sir, I recognize your voice."

"Sorry to be calling so late, cher, but there's been some trouble. Please go wake your father."

"OK." Phoebe turned and found her father already standing there. She handed him the phone. "Mr Pailet." Then she retreated to the refrigerator for a glass of milk.

Her father spoke very briefly, listened mostly, then asked about a location.

Henderson's Wharf was no longer a working wharf since the hurricane had destroyed it twenty years before, but everyone still called the spot Henderson's Wharf.

"OK, Achilles," her father said. "Me, I'm there as soon as I get the boat in the water, eh?" He hung up.

"What's wrong?" Phoebe asked.

"There's a boy, one of the DryadOil boys, him's done gone missing and people's afraid he ended up in the water. The sheriff, he done asked all the fishermen in the area to help out with the search. I'm going." He started back

96

to his bedroom.

"Was it one of the workers?" Some of the derrick roughnecks got rowdy sometimes and ended up in the strangest places round Port Charmant.

"No. This boy is a high school boy. Him and some friends, they were fishing and cooking out tonight by Henderson's Wharf."

Phoebe was afraid to ask. "Wh-who is missing?"

"Mark Chenier. Do you know him, cher?"

Panic filled Phoebe's chest. "He's in my class. Papa, can I come help?"

"No, cher." His tone was gentle but firm. "It could be bad."

Phoebe had never seen a drowning victim, but she'd heard stories about them. And about people the 'gators had gotten, too. "Please, Papa."

"And who's gonna stay with Shiloh, with your mama off to work tonight?"

"We could drop him off at Granmere's."

He put his hands on her shoulders and looked her in the eye. "No, cher. You will stay here with your little brother. We find something out about your friend, I call you soon as I can. My word." He kissed her forehead.

Phoebe stood on the porch, watching her father's joe boat make its way down the bayou. The running lights looked like a swarm of fireflies against the slate black surface of the water.

I shouldn't have yelled at Mark today in front of all those people. Maybe he was so upset, he wasn't careful. You have to be careful in the bayous.

Malevolent spirits were said to roam the bayous, hunting for the unwary. Phoebe looked up at the cluster of stars in the sky, spotting her natal constellation, Pisces. She saw the Milky Way and remembered why the Cajuns called it the *Chasse Gallerie*. It was said to be made up of hunters and dogs eternally fated to go chasing across the night skies after a quarry that could never be caught.

Phoebe didn't know how much of the old stories she believed, but she knew that people did vanish in the bayous and were never seen again. *Don't let that happen to Mark!*

She sat on the porch swing, staring anxiously at the water that looked thick as black Jell-O. As the cold electricity thrilled out from her stomach and filled her, the edges of her vision began to dim and blur. This time Phoebe didn't fight against the *avartisment*'s approach. She welcomed it, keeping Mark uppermost in her mind. "Show me where he is," she whispered. "Show me..."

...Mark wasn't in the water. He wasn't in a boat. Low walls surrounded him, and the dank smell of earth reminded Phoebe of a crypt. She'd been to the family burial vaults for funerals, and they all smelled the same — dank and raw.

She tried to call out to him, but her voice died somewhere along the way.

He was afraid. Shifting round inside his prison, he pounded on the rough wooden door with his fists. "Let me out! Natalie! Hunter!"

The effort of maintaining contact was

draining. Phoebe felt incredibly tired. She pushed herself, until she filled his body and felt the rough wood under Mark's fists as he pummelled the door. His head hurt, and a headache had worked its way up from his shoulders into the base of his skull.

Phoebe peered into the vision harder, trying to force herself past the limits.

"Help!" Mark shouted.

Phoebe tried to fill him with comforting feelings, but he was too frightened to feel them. Mark, it will be OK. I'll find—

"Wake up, Phoebe."

Blinking, she realized that she'd been sleeping on the porch swing. Her mother and father stood over her.

"Girl," her father said, "have you been out here all night?"

Phoebe sat bolt upright. "Did you find Mark?"

Her father shook his head. "We look all night, cher, but we didn't find anything. The sheriff and his men, we don't think we're going to find him."

Cold fear tried to fill Phoebe but she

angrily pushed it back. "Papa, he's not dead. I saw him."

"Round here, cher?"

"Not here. Somewhere else." Phoebe tried to remember. *How much of it was dream and how much of it was vision?* She wasn't sure. Quietly, she described how the visions had started coming to her since yesterday, and that her grandmother had helped her start to learn to focus them.

Her mother and father were attentive. There were no questions about the *avartisments*. Granmere had told them Phoebe would have the power and they'd believed her.

"This place where you saw the boy," her father said, "do you know it?"

"No." Phoebe felt frustrated. "But if I saw it again, I think I would."

"I talk to the other fishermen today," he said. "If they know of such a place, we send someone to check it out."

Phoebe stared at the water, trying to use the power again to find Mark, but she only sensed emptiness.

"Come," her mother said. "Help me fix breakfast. Your papa, he's been up and been cold all night. It's time to get something warm in his belly."

Phoebe went into the kitchen and started the chicory coffee.

"That boy," her mother said, "his girl-friend came into the emergency room last night screaming and carrying on. Dr Means, he had to sedate her."

"Natalie?"

Her mother nodded as she put a tray of rolls into the oven. "I believe that was her name."

"I should call her," Phoebe said. "I'll be right back." She went into her room and looked up Natalie's number in the high school phone book. Until the arrival of DryadOil, they'd never had anything like that. She found the number and dialled.

Natalie's mother answered the phone and talked only briefly. When Phoebe mentioned that she had called to tell Natalie that Mark was alive, her mother ran to get her.

"Hello," Natalie said a few minutes later.

She sounded stressed out and distant. "Phoebe? Mother said you called about Mark?"

"I just wanted you to know he's alive," Phoebe said, uncertain about how to proceed.

"Where is he? I want to see him." Natalie's voice was still frantic.

"I'm not sure."

"What?"

"I saw him in a vision," Phoebe explained. "He was in a small room. It was dark. The walls were cement. Do you know any place like that down by Henderson's Wharf?"

"A vision!" Natalie exploded. "You saw Mark in a dream and you tell me he's OK? He's trapped somewhere in the dark, but he's OK? Is this some kind of sick joke?"

"Natalie, calm down," Phoebe said. "I have these powers. Sometimes, I can see things—"

"You're seeing things now, Phoebe Arceneaux! You've got to be the biggest jerk I've ever met." The phone clattered against something hard.

A man's voice came over the phone next. "This is Natalie's father. I don't know what you're trying to pull, or why you'd want to hurt my daughter, but don't you ever call here again." The phone slammed down.

Phoebe's face burned as she stared at the dead phone in her hand. "She didn't believe me," she said to her mother.

"They're from the outside, cher," her mother said. "They don't know some things can exist despite them believing they don't."

"I can't blame her, Mama. Two days ago, I didn't believe either. Then there was the snake and those warnings and seeing Mark in that, that cement cell. Now I believe, but I don't know what I'm supposed to do."

"Maybe there's nothing you can do, cher."

"No. I'm certain I'm supposed to do something," Phoebe murmured to herself as she poured a cup of hot coffee. "Mark is out there somewhere, alone and scared, and maybe hurt. I'm not going to let him down."

Phoebe hurried to her room to get dressed. It was time for her to talk to Sheriff Langsdale. *He grew up here. He knows Granmere and he's seen proof of her powers. He'll listen. He just has to!*

CHAPTER NINE

*Nimble Mercury is dancing round, speeding
ahead of the Sun in your natal sign. Pisces
love mysteries but your vivid imagination
can run away with you. Don't let Mercury
fool you into thinking you should be the
bearer of good news. Leave that to someone
else while you dig for more clues.*

"So you seen this here boy in a vision?"
Sheriff Langsdale said. He was a big man,
broad and beefy. His full beard was shot
through with grey.

"Yes," Phoebe answered. She felt small
and lost in the big office. A ceiling fan
whirled slowly overhead, and the slanted
blinds looked out over the community park
across the street behind the police
department.

105

Sheriff Langsdale let out a long, tired breath. "We've been combing that area for hours, and we haven't found anywhere like what you described."

"Then he's not there," Phoebe said. "Look somewhere else!"

"Cher," the sheriff said, "I know your granmere a long time. Since I was a boy and she had me sell my first two warts. And these visions you're talking about, I know such things exist."

"Granmere helped find Rose Allemande's little brother a few years ago," Phoebe pointed out.

"I know, and ever'body done figure they never see that baby again. She found others, too. Some living and some dead, and she knew which they was before we got to them."

"Then why won't you listen to me?"

"I *am* listening, cher." Sheriff Langsdale took a handkerchief from his pocket and wiped his florid face. "But you're not giving me anything I can work with. Until I know more, I got to start the search where he was last seen. You understand? His mama and papa, they're calling pretty regular up here, too. I tell them I'm pulling the search party out of Henderson's Wharf, they going want to know why. I got to have a good reason."

Frustrated, but not seeing any way clear of the argument, Phoebe remained quiet.

"Listen to me," Sheriff Langsdale said. "You come up with something more, like maybe where this boy is, I go check it out personal. OK?"

"Yes," Phoebe said with a huge sigh.

The sheriff's swivel chair squeaked as he got up and walked round the cluttered, scarred desk. He patted her on the shoulder. "I know you feel bad. That boy, he has a lot of pretty girls feeling bad about him."

Phoebe had to clamp her jaw shut tight to keep from saying anything. Politely, she thanked the sheriff for his time and walked into a small, narrow hallway full of the thick smell of a lemon-scented air freshener that made her want to gag.

She glanced at the wall clock above the water fountain and saw that it was after ten.

She'd waited an hour to see the sheriff. Still unwilling to go to school and knowing her parents would be upset with her, she wasn't sure what she was going to do.

Phoebe leant over to take a drink from the fountain and was instantly mesmerized by the fluid surface of the water. She reached for the feeling, hoping to get another glimpse of Mark, but it evaded her. When she straightened up, she noticed a collection of wanted posters thumbtacked to the wall.

A man with a broad face and thick beard stared out at her with hard eyes. Below was information that he was wanted for smuggling. A note taped to it described the four-wheel drive van he'd last been seen driving. *He doesn't have the beard anymore, just the moustache.* But she couldn't quite place where she'd seen him before. The power inside her coiled restlessly.

"Miss Arceneaux!"

Startled, Phoebe looked back to the sheriff's office and saw him pulling his jacket on, preparing to leave. "Yes?"

"You see that cousin of yours, you tell him

this from me. If he's going to be doing those tours, he's gonna have to get him a licence like all the rest."

Confused, Phoebe said, "You must be thinking of a Thibodeaux. They're the ones cashing in on the tourist rentals at the cabins."

"Thibodeaux, Arceneaux, what's it matter? You're all as thick as thieves. All I know is that TiChance guar-awn-tees a 'gator." He tipped his Stetson and said, "You send your granmere my regards."

Phoebe nodded and walked through the door out on to the steps. She was afraid for TiChance. Now she knew what he was doing in the swamp the other night so late. *I'll tell Papa. He can talk to TiChance.*

She started down the steps, then the vision swooped down on her without warning, yanking her up to—

—*Mark, who was struggling with the wooden door. The room was more illuminated now, so Phoebe knew the vision was no longer from the night. Maybe it was even taking place now!*

"Help! Someone help me! I think I'm going to be sick."

He hit the door again but the effort was much weaker, more dispirited.

Phoebe heard other noises this time. Of animals, rustling. Birds crying out. She could hear—

—the sound of a car horn right in front of her!

Phoebe thrust out her hands and felt the hot metal against her palms as her mind registered the sounds of tyres skidding. She was pushed backwards, off her feet. Landing with bruising force, she was stunned for a moment.

"Oh my god!" a man said as he helped her to her feet. "What were you thinking? You just stepped off that kerb like you didn't even see me." A crowd started to gather.

"I didn't see you," Phoebe said weakly. "I'm sorry. I wasn't thinking. I'm sorry."

"This could have been a terrible tragedy," the man admonished.

"I know. I'm all right. Thank you." Phoebe walked back to the kerb and hurried away from the people and the man. Her mind was focused on Mark and how to find him.

Granmere! She can help me.

Phoebe ran for the docks. Someone down there would be willing to give her a ride to her grandmother's.

An hour later, Phoebe leapt expertly from the prow of the joe boat to the dock in front of her grandmother's house. Her long skirt whirled round her legs. She turned to wave to Mr Sandusky, who'd given her a ride, and thanked him.

Mr Sandusky, nut-brown, shirtless and lean in overalls waved, then revved the engine and sped away.

Phoebe ran up the hill but her grandmother wasn't in the house when she got there. She called for her, frantic for a moment, then heard her out in the garden. When she rounded the house, she saw her grandmother standing in the middle of the ruined garden.

The old woman was listening intently.

"Granmere?" Phoebe asked, approaching slowly.

"Shush, cher."

Phoebe quietly stood by her.

"You hear them animal noises?" Granmere asked. "Some of them, they ain't no swamp creatures I know of."

Phoebe couldn't hear anything out of the ordinary. She knew her grandmother's hearing was talked about by several of the fishermen. She knew things, they said, that were only whispered on the wind. Maybe it was some sort of compensation for her impaired eyesight.

"But that's not what you're here for, is it, cher? It's that boy, that one who's missing, eh?"

Phoebe was only mildly surprised that her grandmother knew. *Mama must have called her.*

"That's why you're missing school."

"It's Mark. I've seen him," Phoebe explained. "In visions. They're getting stronger, but I don't know where he is. I'm afraid something is going to happen to him."

Surprisingly, her grandmother nodded. "I think so, too. There's not much time. Come here and take my hand, and listen to them animals."

"What's that—?"

"Hush and do as I say." The hard tone in her grandmother's voice startled her. Automatically, Phoebe took her hand. "Now breathe out. Don't worry about getting air back in. It'll do that natural-like. But you need to be receptive if we're gonna find this boy."

Phoebe breathed. She felt it pulling at her, a slim tendril from the east that bored into the centre of her mind.

"You feel it, cher?" her grandmother asked. "The pull?"

"Yes."

"You thinking of this boy's face?"

"Yes."

"Let me see."

Phoebe felt something tug at the tendril.

"This one, he is blond and blue-eyed, with glasses and a clean face, eh?"

Blinking her eyes open, Phoebe looked at her grandmother. The pull disappeared. "How did you know?"

"I saw him in your mind, cher." Her

grandmother looked at her. "This gift you have, there are many things about it that you have still to learn. You have shut it out so long, you are behind in what I could have shown you."

"Tell me what I have to do."

"Look inside yourself, cher," her grandmother said. "What you need is there."

"Can't you find him?"

"No. You are the one linked to him. Not me." She paused. "Take the *pirogue*, cher. Go and find him. I'll be here listening for you. But go now, there isn't much time left."

Less than fifteen minutes later, Phoebe was poling the *pirogue* round Hatton's Bend when she felt the tug again. Only for a moment. Then it was gone.

Drawing the pole back into the *pirogue*, she sat back in the stern and closed her eyes. She'd put on a flannel shirt, jeans, and hiking boots she'd left at her grandmother's during one of her frequent stays, and the breeze cooled her in the shadows of the cypress. She concentrated again, seeking Mark.

"Focus on the pull," she told herself. She

kept her eyes closed and imagined that the force was like a flashlight beam directed at her face. "Feel it, *feel* it!" Slowly her face began to warm, and she could feel the pull. Then she sensed it lock. Like a tractor beam, she could feel it leading her.

Slowly Phoebe opened her eyes, making sure to keep contact with Mark's location. The trail led off to the east, down a narrow channel that she couldn't remember ever travelling.

She only hesitated for a moment. *Mark's there, but until I can prove it, I'm not going to be able to help him. And if I leave now, I might not be able to find him again.* She checked the *pirogue*'s stores. Besides two life jackets, there were also two flashlights in working order, a first-aid box, a flare gun, trail mix, and a canteen of water. All of it was contained in a small backpack.

All right. It's now or never. She took up the pole again. The vision was stronger this time, crossing over until she could feel Mark again. He was still well, but he was in pain that felt...

...rough from the rope round his wrists, but he kept working it against the door frame. The friction was making the chafe marks worse, but he was near panic. He still didn't know who had kidnapped him or why, Phoebe felt, but he'd heard people on the other side of the door. Also, the bird cries hadn't stopped.

The sound of a truck engine rattled through the room, and the stench of diesel slid under the door frame. Voices outside came nearer.

Mark stopped working the rope between his wrists and crouched down on his knees on the dirt-encrusted floor so he could peer through the crack under the door. A pair of boots halted right outside the door. A key turned in a lock, then the door came flying open, thudding painfully into Mark and sending him reeling.

The man that strode through the door with the gun in his fist was the same moustached man Phoebe had seen in her earlier visions. "You awake, kid?" the man asked as he entered the room. Behind him was a white *vehicle with mud splattered on its sides.*

Mark faced the man, breathing hard, afraid but unwilling to show it. Phoebe was proud of him, but feared for him at the same time. "What's going on?" he demanded. "Why did you guys bring me here?"

"Shut up," the man snarled. He slapped Mark backhanded. Mark fell backwards, catching his leg on something sharp.

The pain cut into Phoebe and severed—

—the contact. *Oh god, don't let me be too late.* Phoebe pushed the fear from her mind and kept the *pirogue* slicing neatly through the swamp. The shadows round her were long and twisted, and the bulrushes partially disguised cottonmouths and alligators alike. She made herself ignore them, thinking only of what might be happening to Mark.

CHAPTER TEN

Over three hours passed before she knew she'd found the right place. The swamp finger she was following ended under a thick copse of cypress trees. The vision's thread that had led her this far was definite. She hadn't had any confusion about it for the last forty minutes.

She poled the *pirogue* into the bank, stepped out, and tied up the boat. When she climbed up the hillside and looked back, she was satisfied that it was well hidden. Dusk was further tinting the already dark sky. It would be night in only minutes.

Hidden behind a gnarled willow tree, Phoebe looked down over the campsite. She'd never been to the area, she was certain, but she'd seen a number of them before.

The campsites had started out with small

mobile trailers that were thirty or forty years old now. They'd been put up on stilts to get them above flood level, then porches had been added, and finally extra rooms. They looked like beehives, and the original trailer structures could only be found if searched for.

Campfires dotted areas of the campsite, and at least three men walked round below, finally heading into one of the larger huts. Phoebe's heart was in her throat. Everything in her screamed that she should get out of there. But the vision stayed her, letting her know that if she left, it would be too late for Mark by the time she got back.

Hang on, Mark. I'm coming.

Quietly, she stopped down the incline, taking her time. It took over five minutes to get to the bottom and it was completely dark when she arrived. But she was certain no one in the camp knew she was there.

As she rounded one of the huts, resting only a metre or so above the ground, she heard the strange rustling and pipping sounds of birds that she'd noticed during the earlier visions.

She felt a tugging at her insides.

Mark. There. The small building was a derelict tanning shed that looked as if it hadn't been used in years. She knew Mark was inside, but she couldn't tell what kind of condition he was in. The cold electricity of the power ran nervously through her stomach. *Don't stop! Keep moving!*

She did, and her moves were quieter and more fluid than she'd ever noticed at any time before. She was a shadow stealing through the camp.

Voice reached her ears and she froze under one of the huts. Only snatches of conversation were decipherable.

"...our only chance...they'll be watching the docks for the van..."

Van! The note on the bulletin board at the sheriff's office flashed in her mind. *And the man with the beard...he was from her visions.* Phoebe was quickly putting the pieces of the puzzle together but she wasn't sure what the end result would be. She held her breath and listened with her whole body.

"...so risky *I* wouldn't give you odds..."

"...but the boy swears he has it all worked out..."

There was silence for a moment.

"...OK with me. Slip thirty-nine is..."

"...agreed on the time...even if the cargo goes straight on to the barge, we'll still be cutting it close..."

When the hand fell on her shoulder, Phoebe almost screamed. Only the fact that her breath froze in her chest stopped her. A hand slid round her mouth as someone wrapped an arm round her and kept her from struggling.

"Don't scream and don't fight, cher," a familiar voice whispered, "and I let you go this minute."

Phoebe nodded. When the hand and arm went away, she turned round and saw TiChance standing there. "What are you doing here?" she asked in a whisper.

"My job," he whispered back curtly. "The question is – what are *you* doing here?"

"I'm here to get Mark."

TiChance blinked at her, perplexed.

"Mark's dead. He wasn't found last night. The swamp, it took him. Maybe a 'gator, too."

"He's here," Phoebe snapped. "And I'm not leaving without him."

"You wrong about that, *cousine*." TiChance glared at her. "You leaving now, before I have to turn you in. These men, they be plenty rough about their business, and they don't allow no trespassers at all."

The door to the hut where the voices had been talking suddenly opened and a man walked out.

TiChance reached for Phoebe and pulled her to cover before she could react. She pressed against him as they hid behind one of the trailer supports next to a tall cypress tree.

The man cupped his hands and lit a cigarette. In the instant of flash, Phoebe recognized him as the moustached man. Then he walked to the pair of four-wheel-drive vehicles parked in the centre of the camp.

"What's going on, TiChance?" Phoebe demanded in a whisper.

"Girl, you best be on about your business. You hightail it now, I forget you were ever here. I'm only giving you this chance because you're my cousin. So you get on out and don't come back."

"TiChance!" the moustached man yelled.

"Go!" TiChance told Phoebe, giving her a push towards the tree line. Then he walked towards the other man.

Oh my god, think, Phoebe. Hurry. She wanted to run so badly she could taste it.

The vision filled her. Mark *was* in that tanning shack. In her mind, she could clearly see him. Abandoning her fear, she let it hone the rest of her senses and keep her adrenaline up. She stole across the intervening distance as quickly as she dared.

The wooden door was formidable and heavily scarred. A simple bolt secured it, and a key was in the door handle. Phoebe tapped on the door quietly, then whispered, "Mark."

There was no answer.

She tried again with the same result. Cautiously, she slid the bolt back and turned the key. Easing the door open, she slipped one of the flashlights from the backpack and stepped inside. Once the door was closed, she flicked the light on.

Mark lay huddled on the floor under a thin blanket. Awkwardly, he raised himself up to a sitting position and lifted a hand to block the glare of the flashlight beam. "Who is it?"

"Phoebe," she replied. *Oh god, look at his mouth.*

Blood had dribbled down his chin from the split lip, and purpling continued all the way to his cheek. "Phoebe?"

"Yes. Can you walk?"

"I don't know. I've cut my leg pretty bad." He tried to get to his feet but failed. "How did you find me?"

"I'll explain later. Right now, we need to get you out of here." She crossed the room and cut the rope on his wrists with the knife from the backpack, then slipped his arm over her shoulders. It took effort to get Mark to his feet, but once he was there he seemed able to hold his own. "Are you ready?"

"I don't want to stay here any more." He gave her a lopsided grin that looked even worse with his bent glasses. "The room service is lousy."

Phoebe smiled. "I know. But you've got to be quiet."

"They're still out there?"

"Yes." Phoebe peered through the door and didn't see anyone. She clicked off the flashlight.

"You're here alone?" Mark asked.

"Yes. I've got a boat waiting."

"I thought maybe you brought the sheriff."

"He wouldn't believe that I knew where you were."

"Oh."

"Come on." Phoebe eased out the door.

"Phoebe, I can't see too well at night. I never have been able to, and circumstances right now haven't helped."

"Take my hand, OK?"

"Sure." He did, and it felt warm and reassuring in hers.

Quickly, quietly, she led him out of the tanning shack. She had no doubt they were running for their lives.

CHAPTER ELEVEN

*F*ive minutes later, they were edging up the hill by the camp.

"Stay down," Phoebe said as they neared the top of the rise. "You stand up, they'll see you against the rest of the bayou tree line."

Mark hunkered down and promptly tripped over a root, yanking her off-balance with him. They went sprawling and ended up near the banks of the water. "Sorry."

"Forget it. Climb into the boat." Phoebe held it steady while he hobbled aboard and sat in the middle at her direction.

She pushed the slender craft into the water until it was thigh-deep so she was sure it wouldn't bottom out. Wet and nervous, Phoebe pulled herself into the boat. She grabbed the pole and started them moving.

"Is there anything I can do to help?" he

whispered.

Phoebe had turned the *pirogue* round and was heading back the way she'd come. Mark made a move to help her paddle but Phoebe gestured for him to stay still. "It's OK, Mark. I can handle it."

Phoebe kept peering over her shoulder, but there seemed to be no sign of pursuit. Glancing forward, she realized the swamp looked very different now, at night, than when she'd come earlier. It was going to be very easy to get lost if she wasn't careful.

For twenty minutes they floated in silence except for the nocturnal sounds of the swamp round them. Then Mark broke the stillness. "How did you find me?"

Phoebe told him she was a Pisces, with Jupiter in the twelfth house and Neptune and Virgo in the third house. "What that all adds up to, I'm not quite sure, but my Granmere says I have the gift of seeing."

Phoebe told him about the individual visions she'd been receiving, which seemed to stun Mark.

"ESP?" Mark asked. "Is that what you're

talking about?"

She shrugged and kept poling. "I guess that name fits, but Granmere says every *traiteur* has some form of it."

"*Traiteur*?"

"Doctor. Or healer." Phoebe found one of the bigger arteries of the bayou and poled them round a spreading willow into its course. The moon peeked out briefly and frosted the water.

"Is that what you're going to be, a doctor?"

She hesitated. "I guess it's a possibility."

Phoebe kept vigilant about the threat of pursuit. Still there were no signs. She looked at Mark, sitting so stiffly in the middle of the *pirogue*.

"Why did those men kidnap you?" she asked.

"I have no idea. I was at Henderson's Wharf with the others. Hunter suggested we play a game of hide and seek. Boys against the girls."

"Sounds like something Hunter would suggest," Phoebe cut in.

"I followed him into the woods and these guys came out of nowhere and grabbed me," Mark continued. "The guy with the moustache hit me with a flashlight and I must have been knocked out because I don't remember how I got here."

"You didn't do anything to them?" Phoebe asked.

He gave a choked chuckle and held up his chafed wrists and pointed to his swollen mouth. "Do I look like I could have given those guys a hard time?"

"No, but you sure can tear up an old woman's garden." Phoebe's words were more harsh than she intended.

Mark looked uncomfortable. "I didn't want to be part of that. Hunter and some of the others... It started out as a dare. None of us knew she was your grandmother." He looked down. "At least, I didn't. Not until later."

"Would it have mattered?"

"Yes." He raised his eyes to meet hers. "I like you a lot, Phoebe. I wouldn't have ever hurt you intentionally."

"If it wasn't my granmere's garden, it would have been someone else's."

"Hunter said it belonged to a witch," Mark murmured. "He and K.J. had everybody all riled up about whether or not we were all going to have a curse put on us." He paused. "I didn't tear down a single thing, and I tried to talk the others out of it."

"But you were there," Phoebe said accusingly. "Why?"

"I don't know," he said, shaking his head in disgust. "I was afraid to disagree. I just wanted the others to like me."

Phoebe suddenly felt sorry for Mark. She realized he was just like her, or Annalee, or every other kid at Port Charmant High – only wanting to be liked, and to fit in.

"Look," she said, softly, "we all make mistakes. God knows, I've made my share."

"I knew I'd made one that night," Mark said. "When I saw they weren't going to stop, I ran away. Some men down at a dock near there saw me, and I just knew we were going to get busted the next day. I even saw their van at the school on Wednesday."

Abruptly, the *pirogue* ran aground. Caught off guard, Phoebe nearly went overboard.

"Hey," Mark said, lifting his feet, "we're taking on water like crazy."

Phoebe knew at once that the *pirogue* was going down. There was no way to bail the water out. She picked up one of the life jackets and handed it to Mark. "Put this on. We're going to have to swim for the bank." She glanced across the water, at the bank twenty metres away.

"What'd we hit?" Mark asked.

"Probably a sunken log," Phoebe said, securing the top of her pack that held her supplies and looping it on to her back. "It's my fault." The water was swirling round her ankles. "I should have been watching better."

"Your first rescue attempt," Mark said, "I wouldn't expect you to get everything right."

"Thanks." His smile was infectious. "Can you swim?"

"Piece of cake." He stepped out of the sinking boat and into the water, wincing sharply when the water hit his injured leg.

Phoebe joined him. The water was cold.

"Look out for snakes and 'gators."

"You had to mention that," he groaned.

They reached the bank without incident, but just as they pulled themselves out of the water the staccato roar of a powerboat engine rumbled across the water.

"Down!" Phoebe ordered, moving behind some brush. Nervously, she glanced out as the *pirogue*'s stern disappeared under the water. *Good. Maybe it won't give us away.*

Mark huddled behind some bushes a couple of metres away.

The black Cris-Craft came into view with a searchlight flaring across the water. Phoebe recognized the boat from the times she'd seen it on the bayou. Then she saw TiChance at the wheel. One of the men shouted and pointed, and the searchlight zeroed in on the sunken *pirogue*. TiChance cut the boat's engine.

"They must be on foot. Now we'll never find them!" the moustached man yelled at TiChance. "You were supposed to be guarding that kid."

"Hey, I—" Before TiChance could say

another word, the moustached man hit him in the mouth with a fist. The third man in the powerboat immediately joined him, giving TiChance a beating.

I've got to do something. They'll kill him. Gathering her courage, Phoebe drew in a deep breath, then let out a banshee wail that froze the two men in mid-punch. Taking advantage of the diversion, TiChance dived overboard and began to swim strongly for the bank.

The second man cursed viciously and pulled out a pistol. He started firing at once. Water jumped up in three places round TiChance.

"Wait," the moustached man ordered, playing the searchlight over TiChance. "Look."

Drawn by the action, half a dozen 'gators slithered off the bank into the water, swimming strongly in the boy's direction.

"The 'gators will take care of that Cajun trash," the moustached man said. "Won't be as many questions from the cops that way. But we've got to find that other boy. Let's go back and get the hounds. Organize a search party."

The engine started again, and the powerboat swept round in a wide arc and headed back the way it had come. When they were far enough out of sight, Mark made a muffled cry of pain.

"Mark?"

"My leg. It's hurt worse than I thought," he said tightly. "I think I broke the wound open when I came ashore."

Phoebe made sure the boat was gone, then hurried to his side. With her flashlight on low, Phoebe examined him and found a bloody patch on the outside of his left thigh. "You did," she said, looking at the torn flesh. "It's a pretty deep gouge. Tear a piece of material off your shirt-tail and hold it over the wound. I'll be right back."

She raced to the water's edge, worrying about TiChance and the 'gators.

She listened for the splashing and tracked him, running along the bank. When she found him, TiChance had a naked fishing blade in his hand and was trying to hold four 'gators at bay while he trod water to keep from drifting towards them.

The electricity moved inside Phoebe as she made herself reach for it. She aimed her thoughts at the 'gators. *Go away! There's nothing for you here! No food! Go! Get out of here!*

At first nothing seemed to happen. Then slowly, one by one, the 'gators lost interest and swam away. TiChance scrambled on to the bank. The knife stayed in his hand.

"That was one close call," he said in a very shaky voice. "Me, I thought I was done for."

Phoebe, tired and angry, faced TiChance. "I don't know what you think you're doing working for those men, but you were nearly killed. They left you here to die."

"I never figured them for shooting me," TiChance said, staring off in the direction the boat had gone. "But them fellas, they gonna come into this swamp and do what they want anyway. It don't hurt none if some of their money finds its way into my pocket."

Phoebe started back towards Mark, only to

find him limping towards her. "I thought maybe you'd need some help," he said, blood streaming down his leg from beneath the makeshift bandage.

"Lie down," Phoebe commanded. "We've got to stop that bleeding first."

"Them fellas," TiChance muttered, backing into the trees, "they done picked the wrong guy to double-cross. They don't know it yet, but they gonna find out soon."

In a flash Phoebe's cousin was gone. She could hear the thud-thudding sound of his feet as he made his way through the tangled mass of trees.

"TiChance!" Phoebe cried. But there was no answer.

"Will he be all right?" Mark asked.

"I don't know." Using her knife, Phoebe cut open his jeans leg and exposed the wound. It was deep and jagged and was bleeding badly now. She cut off the rest of his shirt tail and made a pressure bandage. "But TiChance knows these swamps as well as anyone. I don't think there's much danger of him getting lost."

Just as she was finishing Mark's bandage, they heard the baying of dogs.

"What was that?" Mark asked.

"Hounds," Phoebe said, pulling at his arm. "Get up. We can't stay here. They'll find us in minutes." She helped him to his feet, then pointed him in the opposite direction from the dogs.

They ran and limped through the confusion of the swamp. Branches slapped at Phoebe's face as she blazed the way. Without warning, the land dipped abruptly and she fell with a small yelp of surprise. The embankment was over two metres high. When she rolled to a stop at the bottom of it, with Mark right behind her, she noticed that they were in an old cemetery that filled a small clearing.

Gravestones and tombs stuck up from the marshy ground at odd angles, and a low-lying fog swirled aimlessly among the shapes. A dark horned owl rested on a gravestone in the shape of a medieval cross. Its yellow eyes blinked menacingly, then the bird took wing and swooped away.

"We're in a graveyard?" Mark asked.

"Yes."

She'd dropped the flashlight when she fell, and saw that it lay a short distance away. She picked it up from the ground and shone it over the grave markers. Most of the family names were Billiot. "I know where we are. Come on. Help is only a short distance away."

"We're not going to make it," Mark said, as the barking dogs got closer and closer. "They're gaining on us."

A dark furry shape suddenly took a defensive stance in front of them.

"Wait!" Phoebe cried, stopping and blocking Mark with her body. "Skunk!" She used her night vision the way her father had taught her, by looking at the animal with her peripheral vision and not focusing directly on it. There, under a drooping willow, was a mother skunk with five little babies. The mother had her black-and-white striped tail lifted in warning. The babies growled in bubbling coughs round her.

"We can go round them." Mark pulled at

Phoebe.

"Maybe we can use her to get away from the hounds," Phoebe said. Her mind raced furiously. The skunk stood her ground. "Find a rock."

"A rock?"

"A rock." Mark handed her a smooth stone and she hurled it through the air. The stone sailed straight and true, thumping into the skunk's hindquarters with enough force to surprise but not hurt her.

The skunk sprayed at once, startling all her babies into doing the same thing. The immediate vicinity was thick with the overpowering odour.

Grabbing Mark's sleeve, Phoebe pulled him into the brush and they broke into a run again. Just as they made the tree line on the other side of the cemetery, the hounds reached the top of the embankment.

"We can't escape," Mark said. "You shouldn't have come. You didn't have to get caught up in this."

Phoebe tugged him into the shelter of a tree. "Keep still. Don't let them see motion.

That's the easiest thing to pick out in the dark. They haven't caught us yet, and it could be they won't."

The hounds came over the top of the levee in an avalanche of chaos. Men with flashlights followed them, cursing and yelling at the dogs. The hounds raced across the cemetery which was less than fifty metres away.

"I can give myself up," Mark whispered. "They don't even have to know you're here." He started to move away.

"No." Phoebe wrapped her arms round him. "Stay."

Suddenly the hounds' baying turned to one of fear and confusion. They stopped where Phoebe and Mark had encountered the skunk and ran in circles, barking furiously.

"Skunk," one of the men yelled. "Stupid dogs ran up on a skunk. They won't be much good now."

After a few abortive attempts to get the dogs back on track, the men gave up. One of them spoke into a walkie-talkie and a few minutes later a powerboat's engine sounded out from the bayou. The men shone their flashlights round the cemetery without finding anything, then left.

"That was great thinking, Phoebe," Mark said. "I'd never have come up with something like that in a thousand years." He hugged her fiercely.

"We were lucky," she said. Suddenly she was aware that his arms were still round her.

He looked into her eyes, not letting go.

She made a small attempt to push away, murmuring, "We have to run."

"Phoebe."

She looked up at him. Slowly, his eyes still looking deep into her eyes, he brought his lips to hers. The kiss was warm. After a moment, she kissed him back and slid her arms round his neck and suddenly—

—she felt his fear. Through the small, round window, looking through his eyes, she saw the moustached man standing at the side of the road, pointing at them and yelling to half a dozen men. They ran for their trucks. It was daylight, so she saw them clearly.

He turned. "They saw us!" he said. And

through his eyes, she saw herself. She was—

—suddenly holding him tightly. Her stomach turned flip-flops. The *avartisment* had seized her without warning.

"Phoebe?" Mark asked. "I'm sorry. I didn't mean to scare you. I just wanted..." He was at a loss for words.

"Not you," she gasped. "It was a vision." She looked at the forest round them. "It's not over, Mark."

"We'll make it," he said grimly.

"Not if we stay here." Regretfully she let go of him and turned to face the trees. "Now if I can only remember the way out."

It was several hours before Phoebe and Mark emerged from the swamp into another clearing and saw the lights of a house up ahead. They'd got lost twice on the way. Phoebe's hair was wet from the humidity and stuck to her head. Leaves, grass and mud clung to her clothing.

Mark wasn't in any better shape and his limp was far worse.

"Who's house is this?" Mark asked.

"A cousin's," Phoebe replied.

"They'll help us?" he asked.

"Yes." *I think so. I hope so.*

A narrow road that was little more than a cart trail led up to the home. Once it had been a house trailer, but rooms had been added on to it, more than doubling its size. The exterior was greyed from age and the elements, and the shutters hung haphazardly.

Phoebe walked up on to the wobbly porch and knocked on the door while Mark managed the steps with effort.

It took a few minutes before the door was opened. An old woman stood there in pyjamas with a scarf round her head. "What do you want?" Her husband stood behind her, a shotgun in his hands.

"It's Phoebe Arceneaux, Mrs Billiot," Phoebe said. "And a friend. Mark Chenier. We need help."

"It's kinda late for you to be out, ain't it?" the old man asked.

"Some people are looking for us," Phoebe said. Quickly she told them of Mark's kidnapping and the fact that he was hurt. When she finished the old couple invited them in.

As the old woman helped Mark get comfortable on the worn sofa in the living room, the old man brought out some hurricane lanterns and lit them. The walls were hung with paint-by-numbers paintings of clowns and Elvis.

Phoebe peeled the material away from Mark's wound and saw the angry red of infection that had already set into the torn flesh.

"That boy there," the old man said, pointing at Mark, "him's tore up pretty bad, you betcha. That wound, he needs help or it's gonna get a lot worse."

"Do you have a phone?" Phoebe asked.

The old woman shook her head. "No, and you can't leave that wound untended, cher. I get you some water. Henri," she said to her husband, "you go send Ike's boy to get Sebastian Polite's truck for these young folk."

The old man nodded and lumbered out of the door.

When the woman brought back a pail of

water, Phoebe dug through her backpack and found a plastic envelope of crushed peach stones. She sprinkled them in the water.

"What's that?" Mark asked.

Phoebe told him. "As it settles, it'll take impurities out of the water, if there are any." After the sediment had drifted to the bottom, she dampened a cloth and cleaned Mark's wound. It was already seeping from the infection. "Do you have any medicine?" she asked the old woman.

"Bearfat, yes. Maybe some fish oil. But nothing to take care of that, cher. Your granmere, she take care of this family any time something bad happens."

Asking the woman to stay with Mark, Phoebe went outside and started looking at the foliage, trying to remember what her grandmother used to make a poultice to draw out infection.

Granmere, I really need you now. I'm so lost, and Mark is hurt so—

"Be still, cher. I am here."

The voice, so clear and close, sounded as if it came from behind her. Phoebe turned, expecting to see her grandmother. But only the night and the forest was there. "Granmere?"

"Listen to me, cher. Open your mind and let the gift bring my voice to your ears."

"Mark needs help," Phoebe said. "I don't know what to do." Quickly she outlined the wound.

"For this, you need knitbone. Do you remember it?"

"No." Phoebe felt close to panic. It would take so long to get help into the swamp.

"It will be OK, cher. This boy you're protecting, we both take care of him now, eh? Here is knitbone." The picture formed in Phoebe's mind. The plant was tall, with a flowering stem and low, large, hairy leaves. *"Knitbone, he can be hard to find this time of year, but you can find him."*

Using her gift, Phoebe sensed the plant nearby. She switched off the flashlight and went for it. In tune with the power now, her night vision seemed much clearer and less confusing than the flashlight beam. She found the knitbone growing down by the bayou and gathered what her grandmother directed.

On the porch, she chopped the stems of the plants and took only the roots. Then she pounded them to pulp in a granite mortar the old woman gave her, and added some alcohol. When she went inside to check on Mark while waiting for the knitbone to marinate, she discovered he was burning up with fever.

His eyes were bright and hard from the temperature, but he grinned at her anyway. "I don't think I'll be running any more hundred-metre dashes for a while."

Phoebe pressed a cool cloth to his forehead. "I'm going to take care of you," she promised. "You just let me do it and don't worry."

He nodded and dozed off.

"That leg," the old woman said, "he looks mighty bad. That infection don't clear up, them doctors in Port Charmant might want to chop it off when he gets to them."

Phoebe nodded. Gangrene was a real threat in the swamp. She returned to the knitbone, used a piece of cheesecloth to strain it, then shook it violently to drain the remaining liquid out. She made a poultice with some clean cloth Mrs Billiot gave her, then went and tenderly wrapped Mark's leg.

"Make sure that wound is clean, cher." Granmere's voice echoed softly in her head. *"That knitbone, it heal a body so quick it heal over dirt if you let it."*

He was asleep when she did it, but he woke up for just a moment, not really aware of anything because of the pain, exhaustion, and fever. Looking at Phoebe, he said, "You owe me another kiss. We weren't really finished with the first one."

Phoebe turned red because Mrs Billiot had overheard him.

"That one," the old woman said, "him's got romance in his eye when he looks at you."

"It's just the fever," Phoebe said. "He already has a girlfriend."

The old woman snorted. "She may have him now, cher, but me, I don't think she have him long."

Phoebe washed Mark's face. She felt bone-tired.

"Cher," Mrs Billiot said, "your beau will be fine on that divan. You, I think, can sleep in this chair." She patted a recliner nearby. "When my Henri gets back, I wake you."

Phoebe mumbled her thanks and sank into the armchair with relief. She fell asleep so quickly that she didn't remember closing her eyes. Her final thoughts were of the latest vision she'd had, of the moustached man and his gang of thugs closing in on her and Mark. Somehow Phoebe knew that she and Mark wouldn't elude them for much longer. She didn't know what else was going to happen, but her power told her that much. What they would do when their pursuers caught up with them, she had no idea.

CHAPTER TWELVE

A third quarter Moon in Scorpio trines up
all the water signs, including yours, Pisces.
You're over-emotional about something
(someone?) and your intuition is telling you
to trust a big hunch. There's some digging
yet to do but whatever sleuthing you're up
to – keep dry-eyed about it.

*B*learily, Phoebe opened her eyes. Shafts of bright morning sunlight streamed through the windows of the old home. Mark was still asleep on the couch.

"Henri got back a while ago," the old woman said.

"What time is it?" Phoebe asked, sitting up.

"A little after six. I let you sleep as long as I could. Your beau, I left him for you to rouse."

Phoebe thanked her, then went to wake Mark. His head felt cooler when she laid her palm against it.

He opened his eyes slowly. "Didn't you sleep?"

"Some. How are you feeling?"

Taking a deep breath, Mark sat up gingerly. "A whole lot better than I did when I went to sleep."

Phoebe removed the poultice to inspect the wound. Incredibly, almost all of the inflammation was gone.

"You done good, cher," Mrs Billiot said. "The healing gift, you've got it like your granmere. She retire, I think you be a good replacement." She patted her arm.

Phoebe fashioned another poultice and put it on Mark's leg. "We need to go," she said. "Mr Billiot's got a boat outside waiting for us, and my parents are going to be as worried as yours."

Mark nodded and shoved himself to his feet. Surprise showed on his face as he put weight on the injured leg. "Wow," he said.

"You can be my nurse anytime."

Phoebe was pleased by the compliment but knew in her heart that once they were back in Port Charmant and Mark was round his oilfield friends again, she would go back to just being a Cajun girl from the swamps.

"I fix you a bite of breakfast," the old woman said, handing Phoebe a picnic basket. "This trip with Henri, it take a little while. You have time to eat."

Phoebe thanked her and gave her a hug, promising to call again, and led the way to the small dock where Mr Billiot was waiting in his *pirogue*.

Mark didn't look happy about the prospect of another boat ride, but said nothing as he took a seat.

"You eat breakfast, eh?" the old man said as he expertly poled them out into the centre of the bayou. "These waters, I been here since I was a boy. They be my friends. I get you home, you betcha."

Phoebe nodded and opened the picnic basket, smelling the delicious odours at once. Inside were rolls and sausages, fruits and cheeses, fresh preserves, and homemade butter. She handed Mark a roll smothered in jam, and another with sausage in the middle.

"You look very pretty," Mark said, taking a bite.

"You're still delirious," Phoebe replied. "I haven't been able to do more than brush my hair this morning."

"Natural beauty," Mark said with a shrug. "It can't be helped."

Phoebe rolled her eyes, but inside she felt wonderful. It would have been a perfect morning if thoughts of the moustached man out there looking for them hadn't kept creeping into her head.

Three hours later, after they had been handed off three different times to other men in boats, each one of them taking them through another bayou to get them closer to home, Mark whispered to Phoebe, "How did they know we were coming? I thought they didn't have any phones."

"Communication out here has been round a lot longer than phones," Phoebe said. "They have their own ways."

The sun was rising high into the blue sky, burning off the last vestiges of rain clouds that had hung on through the night. Mr Crenshaw, their latest ferryman, pulled them in close to a ramshackle dock where another man sat on the running board of an ancient Dodge pick-up that had once been blue-green. Red fuzzy dice hung from the rear-view mirror .

"TiJean D'Arnot," the man said as he got up from the pick-up, "that is my name." He stuck out a hand.

Phoebe introduced herself and Mark. "Can you drive us into Port Charmant?" she asked.

The man gave her a wry grin. "That, cher, I cannot do." He shrugged expressively. "The licence, she is not mine. Those tests they give, them confuse me. But you, you're welcome to take my truck."

Phoebe accepted the keys. "But what about you? Will you need to go to town?"

"Me, I take a ride with my good friend, Tank." Mr D'Arnot pointed to the man in the *pirogue*. "He and I, maybe we fish, maybe we just tell lies to each other this morning."

He said goodbye and clambered down into the waiting boat.

The pickup's door creaked as Mark opened it.

"Do you want to drive?" Phoebe asked.

"Not with this leg," Mark answered, struggling into the passenger side. "I think the clutch would about kill me."

Phoebe hopped in the truck and with a last wave to the two men who'd helped them, let out the clutch and took off across the dirt road. The potholes made it impossible to get any kind of speed up.

"How far to town?" Mark shifted, trying to get comfortable.

"It's ten, maybe twelve miles to the highway," Phoebe answered. "Only a couple more till we get to Port Charmant." She'd been surprised to learn how far away she'd gotten from Blackcat Bayou during her search for Mark.

"The first pay phone you see," Mark said, "I'd like to stop and call my parents. Find out where they are."

Phoebe nodded. "I need to call my own."

"It's so beautiful out here," he said, looking out of the truck window. "I can see why your people stayed."

"My people?" Phoebe raised an eyebrow. "You make us sound like some foreign tribe."

"Well, you certainly are a tribe," he replied. "We saw that in the swamp, with everyone knowing everyone else, using some sort of magical form of communication. And you with your visions – well, I think that qualifies as very foreign – at least to me."

Phoebe kept her eyes on the road. "Is that bad?"

"No." Mark touched her arm gently. "It's interesting. Different. I like it."

"What about Natalie – would she like it?" The words were out of Phoebe's mouth before she could stop them. She regretted them immediately.

"Ah. Natalie." Mark took his hand away and slumped down in his seat with a huge sigh. "I'd almost forgotten about her."

Phoebe wanted to kick herself for ever mentioning Natalie's name. "Look, I don't know why I said that," Phoebe began. "I guess I'm just—"

"Stop!" Mark suddenly cried, pointing ahead. "There's Hunter! He's got a phone in his car. I can use it to call my parents!"

Phoebe put her foot on the brake so hard they were both thrown forward and saved only by the seat belts. The pick-up turned sideways in the middle of the two-lane highway and stalled. On the other side of the road, Phoebe saw Hunter standing beside his dark jade Mitsubishi 3000GT. Her sudden stop had caught his attention, and that of the men he was talking to.

Mark had opened his door and was about to get out when he froze. Suddenly he jumped back into the pick-up. "Drive! Now!"

"What's wrong?" Phoebe turned the key but the engine just turned over without catching. She kept trying.

"Hunter's talking to the guys who kidnapped me!" Mark said.

Phoebe glanced into the rear-view mirror and saw the moustached man. He pointed at the pick-up truck and yelled to the men with him. Two of them raced towards the pick-up on foot, guns in their hands. The others loaded themselves into the white van that had been partially hidden in the bushes on the side of the road.

"It's the vision! It's coming true!" Phoebe cried.

"Duck!" Mark yelled.

With a sudden burst of power, the engine caught and the pick-up bolted forward. In the rear-view mirror, Phoebe saw the men start firing their guns. One of the bullets smashed through the back glass, tore down the wildly-swinging fuzzy dice, and pierced the windshield, leaving spider-web cracks behind.

"My god," Mark gasped, "they're trying to kill us!"

"But why?" Phoebe's heart was pounding a million times a second. She kept her head pressed against the steering wheel, praying a bullet wouldn't find her.

"I don't know, I don't know," Mark screamed. "Just get us out of here!"

Their pick-up rounded a curve and for a

moment they were out of range.

"If Hunter's in on this thing with them, then that means he set me up to be kidnapped," Mark rasped, staring out of the pick-up's shattered back window.

"Wasn't the whole picnic his idea?" Phoebe asked, struggling to keep the speeding pick-up on the road.

Mark nodded. "And the game of hide and seek. He planned the whole thing."

"Do you see them yet?" Phoebe asked, keeping the accelerator floored as they sped over the Chivalry Bridge.

"They're rounding the corner now!" Mark's voice was hoarse from shouting.

"Usually there's a cop here running a speed trap." Phoebe slammed her fist against the wheel. "Why isn't he here today?"

Off in the distance they could see the banners hanging over downtown Port Charmant. "Look, Mark," Phoebe cried. "See the banners? The parade's today."

"That's where the sheriff is." Mark squeezed Phoebe's arm. "We're saved!"

Without warning, the white van came

alongside them and rammed the pick-up, knocking it up on to the kerb.

"Oh no!" Phoebe hit the brake and turned at the first street she came to. Unable to stop as quickly, the van shot through the intersection, followed by another truck and Hunter's car.

Realizing where she was, Phoebe turned into an alley and sped towards the ramshackle two-story building at the other end. Pulling the pick-up to a stop, she barked, "Get out!"

She ran on wobbly legs to the door at the back of the building and opened it. "Mr Zanuck never locks his door," she hissed, pulling Mark into the warehouse. At the far end of the alley, the van was just turning into view.

"What is this place?" Mark's voice was as shaky as hers as he glanced nervously round the dark recesses of the warehouse.

"It's Mr Zanuck's costume shop," Phoebe whispered, struggling to lock the door behind her. Her hands were shaking so hard she could barely do it. "Hallowe'en and Mardi

Gras are his busiest times of the year, but he also does weddings and all kinds of parties."

Shelves lined the walls, filled with bolts of cloth, plastic containers of buttons, sequins, and zips, and spools of thread. One rack of old costumes stretched the entire length of the room. "Grab a costume. Maybe we can disguise ourselves long enough to get help."

Phoebe yanked a floor-length pink satin gown covered in bright sequins off the rack. "Don't put it on here, they could find us. There's a gas station round the corner we can use." Phoebe also grabbed a pair of high heels.

"How about a wig?" Mark grabbed a box labelled **WIGS**.

"Get something totally gross or weird," Phoebe directed. "The more we change our looks, the better chance we have."

He tossed her a beehive hairdo done in silvery-white, then took a colonial ponytail in black for himself. "If I weren't so scared, this would be fun."

Something thudded against the door and

Phoebe nearly dropped her costume. "Oh my god, they're here!" she hissed. The second time the thump was louder and harder.

Phoebe grabbed a feathered mask for herself and a black domino mask for Mark. "Run," she gasped, sprinting for the other door. "I hope they haven't gone round the front."

Mark opened the door and they peered out cautiously. "Let's go."

Phoebe ran, surprised at how empty the street was. She didn't stop running until they reached the service station. Mark bolted into the men's room while she charged for the ladies.

Phoebe hurriedly undressed and put the costume on. She was struggling to fix the wig in the streaked mirror when Mark knocked on the door.

"C'mon, Phoebe," he whispered. "They're coming out of the dress shop now."

Phoebe slipped on the mask and went outside.

Clad in the skintight pants, buccaneer boots with rolled tops, a ruffled white dress shirt with belled sleeves, and wearing the dark wig in a ponytail and the domino mask without his glasses, Mark Chenier looked as if he'd just stepped off a pirate ship.

"Well, you finally got your wish," Phoebe said, remembering an earlier conversation.

"What do you mean?" Mark asked.

"You're now a pirate."

A wry grin spread across his face. "A very scared pirate. Come on." Mark glanced over his shoulder at where the moustached man and four of his gang were walking round, talking to a few stragglers on the street. "I wish I knew what these guys wanted with me." He took her by the hand.

Suddenly the power swelled inside Phoebe and brought her to her knees. She saw...

...a large white truck parked at a wooden jetty near her grandmother's house. The headlights glared out over the still bayou water. Her hand still hurt from the rough wood of the fence, and she realized she was inside Mark's memories of the night her grandmother's garden was wrecked. Mark was afraid the men in the truck and the van

might have seen him and he ducked into the brush.

At the door of the van was the man with the moustache. He pointed towards the brush where Mark was hiding, just as a large wire cage was carried out of the big truck. Inside the cage were a large number of colourful birds, all making rustling and pipping noises. Then Mark was running, worried that—

"—they *did* see me that night." Mark stared at her, holding her hand in his. "You just made me see. I thought they did, but I wasn't sure. And I sure don't recall seeing everything that night as vividly as we just did now."

"It's the power," Phoebe said, checking over her shoulder. The moustached man and his gang were crossing the street. "We've got to get out of here."

"Slowly," Mark advised. "So they don't recognize us."

Phoebe made herself walk slowly despite the way her heart thudded inside her chest. "Those were birds in those cages," she whispered.

"Parrots," he agreed. "Obviously they were smuggling them in. I had a friend in Hot Springs who used to collect birds. A lot of them get really expensive, and it's hard to get many of them without spending thousands of dollars."

"So they're trafficking in illegal birds."

Mark looked at her. "It's the only thing that makes sense. Hunter wanted us to destroy your grandmother's garden that night as a diversion while they shipped the birds in and out. They had to go right by your grandmother's but if her interest was on the garden—"

"—she might not pay too much attention to who was going up and down the bayou," Phoebe said, finishing his sentence.

They heard the brass band thumping and blaring in the distance. Then Phoebe saw the fire chief's car leading the parade a block away. "Look!" Phoebe pointed. "Our float!"

The two of them hurried to get a close-up look at their handiwork.

"It looks fantastic," Mark cried. "Like a

giant cake."

The model bayou covered with gnarled cypress roots was impressive. With the sun shining down on it, the foil river looked almost real. Dozens of kids dressed as old Acadians and wearing traditional masks based on the ones Annalee had brought waved at the crowd. At the far end, K.J. Carmichael and Natalie Royster posed as king and queen of the float, wearing red capes with fake ermine trim. Both of them sported crowns and gold sceptres.

Freshly cut pine trees stood along the fake bank and looked as if they'd grown there. The banner along the side of the float read, "PORT CHARMANT HIGH presents GUMBO SOUP: A History of the Seasoning of Port Charmant".

"We're blown," Mark said, looking over his shoulder.

Phoebe saw one of the moustached man's thugs emerging from the ladies' room with her clothing. Grabbing the clothes and throwing them down, the moustached man pointed at her and Mark.

"Run!" Mark said, pushing her into motion. Down the block the fire chief's car turned the corner, following the path that had been laid out for the parade.

Phoebe dodged a red and white sawhorse being used as a barrier and paused to kick her shoes off. She ran faster in bare feet.

"What are we going to do?" Mark huffed, running along side her. "I haven't seen a cop yet, and I don't want to get anyone involved that can't shoot back at these guys if it comes to that."

"The float," Phoebe said. "They won't dare start anything in public." She sprinted for all she was worth, lifting her dress as she ran, the concrete sidewalk tearing at her feet.

Luckily the float wasn't going fast enough to leave them behind. Phoebe scrambled up on it as it made the wide corner, then turned and offered her hand to Mark.

He was limping badly.

"Come on!" she shouted. "It's our only chance!"

Other high school students joined her on the float, thinking it was some kind of game.

They cheered Mark on as he made a stronger effort. He put his hand in Phoebe's. Leaning back, she helped pull him up on to the float, aided by a couple guys she recognized from the football team.

"Hey, who are you two?" Missy Blume asked. She was dressed as a Southern belle.

Phoebe peered into the fiery blue eyes behind Mark's domino mask and they reached a silent agreement to keep things quiet. The knowledge that Mark was really alive would prevent them from getting to Sheriff Langsdale as quickly.

Pitching her voice high, Phoebe said, "We're the ghosts of Mardi Gras Past."

"Right," Missy said. "Now, really, who are you guys?"

"The ghosts of Mardi Gras Past," Mark insisted, also in a high voice also. "It wouldn't be a party without us."

"You," Missy said to Mark, "look like Zorro."

He smiled, then grabbed Phoebe's elbow and ushered her to the centre of the float.

Phoebe searched the crowd gathered on

both sides of the street. The moustached man and his thugs were having no problem slipping through the people and keeping pace with the float. She was hoping to glimpse the sheriff or one of his deputies. Nothing was ahead of them except the docks along the bayou.

"Slip thirty-nine," she whispered.

"What?" Mark asked. He was staring at Natalie.

Phoebe jabbed him a little extra hard in the ribs with her finger. "I heard those men who kidnapped you talking about slip thirty-nine."

"You're sure?"

She nodded.

"Stay here, OK?"

"Where are you going?"

"Just stay right here." Mark walked away, heading straight for Natalie, who was waving at the crowds but not really smiling. She looked sad.

Of course, Phoebe thought. *She still thinks Mark is lost. Well, maybe she has a heart after all.*

Unwilling to watch the reunion, Phoebe turned away and sat down on the edge of the wood frame supporting the plaster riverbank. The float riders kept throwing confetti into the crowd of spectators.

Phoebe tried to prepare herself for Mark going back to Natalie, but she suddenly felt something moving under her. She cocked her head and heard a pipping and rustling that was familiar.

She turned and found a section where two pieces of the bank joined together. Slipping her hands in the seam, she opened the crack so she could look in.

Her heart jumped into her throat when she saw a row of beady eyes looking back at her. "What on earth—?"

A heavy hand fell on her shoulder. She turned, expecting to find Mark there, wanting to tell him that the hollow base of the float was filled with smuggled birds.

It wasn't Mark.

Hunter Reed was dressed in a French admiral's uniform with no mask. A cruel smile crept across his lips. "Surprise!"

CHAPTER THIRTEEN

"**D**on't try anything and you won't get hurt," Hunter said. His grip on Phoebe's arms told her he was definitely willing to hurt her.

Phoebe looked back at Mark and Natalie. K.J. and Natalie were still at their places but Mark had disappeared.

"C'mon," Hunter said, walking her to the edge of the float. "We're getting off."

Phoebe wanted to scream but she knew Hunter would hurt her before anyone on the float realized it wasn't part of the festivities.

"I don't think so," a calm, cool voice said.

When Hunter spun round, he brought Phoebe with him.

Standing like a swashbuckler from centuries ago, Mark faced Hunter. His blue eyes blazed from behind the domino mask. "Let her go," Mark ordered.

"Mark?" Hunter tried to act surprised. "When did you get back?"

Mark took a step closer and growled, "I thought you were my friend. Now I'm disgusted that I ever knew you."

"Yeah, well, that's your problem." Hunter's voice hardened. "Now you're both coming with me, or I'm going to accidentally fall off this float and hurt her really bad."

Marshalling her courage, Phoebe stuck her foot behind Hunter's and bucked backwards.

Hunter fell off balance but came up quickly. His training on the football field had made him strong and fast. He launched a hard-knuckled fist at Phoebe. The crowd booed in appreciation, thinking that the fight was staged, that two warriors were competing for the affection of a Cajun queen.

Mark stepped in without hesitation and blocked the blow with a forearm, then shoved Hunter backward. "Stop it!"

"No way," Hunter said. "You two have cost me plenty." He stood near the edge of the fake bayou, then reached down and ripped a cypress root loose.

"Mark! Look out!" Phoebe screamed.

Whirling, Mark grabbed a sword from a nearby guy dressed as a musketeer. The sword was made of metal but the edge was blunt. Still, it glinted as Mark brought it round and parried the cypress root in Hunter's hands.

Hunter snarled in rage and swung again and again. But everywhere he tried to strike Mark, the sword was there.

Out of the corner of her eye, Phoebe saw one of the moustached man's thugs trying to climb up on the float. She pulled one of the small pine trees loose and dropped it into the man's face. Taken by surprise, the man fell into the street, wrapped round the tree.

Phoebe spun in time to see Mark's injured leg slip from under him.

Hunter was on him in a moment, drawing back a fist to drive into Mark's face as he lay pinned.

"*No*!" Phoebe leapt on to Hunter's back and grabbed the fist with both hands. They struggled and she pulled him to the side. When he pushed her away and started to hit her, Mark punched him in the face with a clenched fist.

Before Hunter could recover, Mark rolled him over on to his face and jacked Hunter's arm up behind his back, freezing him painfully in place. Hunter cursed and tried to get up, but Mark moved the arm meaningfully. "This can go easy or hard," Mark said. "Your choice."

The other kids started to crowd in now, wondering what was going on, because they knew this wasn't part of their act. The crowd was cheering the pirate's victory.

Except for the moustached man and his men.

"Mark," Phoebe said, "the birds are in the false bottom of the float. They're headed for—"

"—Slip thirty-nine," Mark finished. "I know. I checked with K.J. because I remembered Hunter was supposed to give some kind of party there after the parade. We've got to stop the float before it gets there."

"But how?" Only one more street remained before the float reached the docks.

Then Phoebe saw Sheriff Langsdale standing beside his car on the right. She waved frantically, but he only waved pleasantly back. "The sheriff!" Phoebe shouted to Mark. "I can't get his attention."

"Use the power, cher." Her grandmother's voice was suddenly inside her head. *"Use the power, and that driver, he listen to you."*

"OK, Granmere." Phoebe pushed through the costumed teenagers heading for the front of the float. She could still see the moustached man and his men keeping pace with them.

"Phoebe! Is that you?" Annalee, who was dressed in buckskins and a wig, caught hold of her arm and peered at her through the mask. "What's going on?"

"Mark's alive, but we're being chased." Phoebe pointed at one of the men closing in on the float. "Don't let that guy on the float. He's one of the guys who kidnapped Mark."

Whirling, Annalee threw her hard rubber tomahawk with astonishing accuracy and hit the man between the eyes. He stumbled and fell back as the crowd roared with laughter.

After all, it was Mardi Gras and anything could happen.

At the cab of the truck, Phoebe leapt down on to the running board. Reaching for the power inside her, she focused it on the driver and ignored the other man in the cab. She didn't know if they were in with Hunter and the moustached man, or not.

Concentrating, she put the suggestion that the next turn was the one to take into the driver's mind. At the corner, he started turning – right into the sawhorses that had been lined up to block the traffic.

"Hey," the guy in the passenger seat shouted. "What do you think you're doing?" He reached for the wheel.

But it was too late to stop it. The oversized truck and flatbed were already committed. They made the turn, leaving the fire chief's car and the brass band that had been in the lead behind in confusion. The other floats came right along after.

Phoebe ran back to where Mark was holding Hunter. The moustached man waved his men towards the float and they closed in.

"We're going to have to do something," Mark said.

Phoebe glanced round wildly and saw TiChance making his way through the crowd. His entire focus was on her. Phoebe waved at him and he waved back. When she pointed at the moustached man, TiChance nodded. He hurried to Sheriff Langsdale's side and started yelling and pointing at the moustached man.

"Give me a hand," Phoebe shouted to Mark and Annalee. She picked up Mark's borrowed sword from where it had fallen and ran to the mock bayou. She jumped down in the middle of it and tore at the foil river.

She rammed the sword blade in between the joints enough to get her fingers in. Then Phoebe started pulling. Annalee and Mark helped her.

"Now we know why Hunter talked his dad into helping out with the float," Phoebe said. "It gave them a way to get the birds to the dock."

"What are you talking about?" Annalee asked.

Just as the moustached man and two of his thugs clambered over the side of the float, the plywood floor gave way. Immediately, a storm of blue, gold, red, green, purple, grey, and indigo birds burst from their prisons and took to the sky. Frightened and confused, the parrots blitzed the costumed teens and scattered them in all four directions across the float.

Abruptly the float screeched to a halt. Evidently the drivers had been through enough confusion.

The moustached man headed for Mark and Phoebe, a gun in his fist.

"Let's go!" Mark said. He grabbed Phoebe's hand and sprinted for the other end of the float. As he reached it, his wig fell off.

"Mark?" Natalie cried, recognizing him. "It's you!"

"Jump," Mark said to Phoebe. The float behind them was less than two metres away. Still holding hands, Phoebe jumped at the same time Mark did. The second float was smaller and shorter. An gigantic clam shell covered the platform atop a small pick-up.

The inside of the clam shell was painted a soft pastel pink, echoed by the pink love seat that sat in the middle of it. Red heart-shaped cushions covered the love seat and spilled into the clam shell floor. Phoebe and Mark landed on the love seat and somehow managed to keep from hitting each other, though they did get tangled up.

The moustached man shoved aside K.J. and Natalie and brought his gun up.

"I wouldn't do that if I was you!" Sheriff Langsdale declared. He held his own gun in two big fists, aimed right at the moustached man's heart.

"OK," the moustached man said. "I'm putting it down. All right?" He put the pistol down and a deputy sheriff stepped up and took it away.

Mark helped Phoebe to her feet and looked at her with concern. "Are you hurt?"

"No." She reached up and took her mask off, conscious of her hand in his. He didn't seem to be in any hurry to let go.

Round them, some of the men in the crowd stepped forward and helped the sheriff and

TiChance round up the last of the crooks. No one got away. Even Hunter was taken into custody.

"Mark!" It was Natalie.

Regretfully, Phoebe pulled her hand from Mark's. "You should go to her."

He nodded, slowly. "I want to thank you for what you've done. I don't know what would have happened to me if you hadn't found me. I owe you a lot."

Phoebe made herself smile even though it felt like her heart was breaking. "You don't owe me anything, Mark. I was just being your friend."

She let Mark help her down from the float, then Phoebe's mother and father, who had been searching for her, swept her into their arms. Her brother Shiloh grabbed her round the waist and squealed, "We found you! We found you! I thought Mr Cottonmouth came back to get you but you're OK!"

Phoebe didn't turn to look at Mark again because she didn't want to see Natalie in his arms.

CHAPTER FOURTEEN

*Mercury is once again in Aries, to be
followed shortly by the Sun. That sun is
shining on you, little fish, and spring will
bring someone's arms round you. Those two
things will make you very, very warm. At
last.*

"Phoebe?"

She turned in the hallway. The school was
filled with the Monday morning chatter that
began every new week, only today there was
much more of it since the Mardi Gras parade
on Friday. Phoebe's heart skipped a beat
when she recognized the voice as Mark's.

He stood in the hallway, holding a package
under his left arm.

"How's your leg" she asked.

Mark nodded. "Good. Doc says I'll be sore

181

for a few days, but rest will take care of it."

"Yes." Phoebe had slept most of the weekend herself, after finishing giving statements to the police and telling stories to relatives.

"Did you hear? They charged Hunter and the moustached man with smuggling, kidnapping, and half a dozen other charges."

"I hope they add attempted murder to that," Phoebe said, thinking back on their terrified flight through the swamps. "And who was that guy anyway?"

"His name, or I guess I should say one of his many names, is Del Veronne. He's a guy with a police record as long as his arm."

Phoebe cocked her head. "But how did Hunter hook up with that slime?"

"Remember when Hunter and his dad took that trip to Brazil round Christmas?"

"How could I forget," Phoebe muttered. "All Hunter ever talked about was Rio."

"Well, apparently Hunter got hooked up with Veronne while he was on vacation. And that's when they set up the smuggling operation."

Phoebe shook her head. "I don't get it. Hunter has everything. Why did he need to do that?"

"Hunter liked the idea of having his own cash. But probably more important – running his own operation. Through his father he had access to the DryadOil docks and with a little local help from guys like TiChance, he was able to help Veronne pull off their scheme."

"I'm glad Hunter's sitting in jail. Maybe it will knock some sense into his head."

Mark sighed. "Hunter only spent a few hours behind bars. His father has him out on bail, but the others are still there."

Phoebe smiled. "Thank god they let TiChance go. I mean, he helped the sheriff catch those guys."

"That's right," Mark agreed. "His testimony will bring down the whole smuggling ring."

"TiChance feels pretty awful about what happened to you. He swears he didn't know."

"I believe him," Mark said.

"So do I," Phoebe replied.

There was a huge moment of silence,

while Mark cleared his throat and stared first at Phoebe, then at the floor and then back at Phoebe.

"I spoke to your grandmother this weekend," he finally said.

"Oh?" Phoebe was surprised. She hadn't mentioned it.

"Yeah, I told her that as soon as I start getting round a little better, I'm going to help her fix her garden. I talked to some of the other guys and they agreed to help me."

"Thanks. I know she'll appreciate it."

Aware of all the attention on them, Mark said, "Can I walk you to your class?"

"Sure."

He fell into step, limping beside her as they started down the hall. "Natalie and I broke up," he said, when they'd got a little distance from the lockers.

Phoebe's heart skipped a beat, but she forced herself to remain calm. "Why?"

"We weren't getting along very well, as you may have noticed. And then this weekend, after everything that happened, I knew I had to do it."

Phoebe kept walking, hardly breathing.

"Look." Mark stopped in the hall and faced her. "I don't know how to say this except – you came for me out there in that swamp, not knowing what you were going to have to face." His blue eyes locked with hers. "Now I'm coming for you, and I'm scared to death because I don't know what you're going to say."

"What do you want me to say?"

For a moment he was silent. "You're not going to make this easy, are you?"

She smiled. "Nope. I had to crawl through mud and 'gators, get sunk, shot at, and almost beaten up for you. Personally, I don't think you have it so rough."

"I've got something for you." He handed her the package he'd been carrying.

Phoebe unwrapped it and found a ship in a bottle inside. On the prow, written in neat lettering, was **PHOEBE, CAJUN PRINCESS.**

"Your grandmother introduced me to your uncle," Mark explained. "I worked hard all weekend to finish it for this morning. It's my first ship in a bottle. I want you to have it."

"Oh, Mark." Phoebe threw her arms round his neck, almost knocking him off balance. He hugged her fiercely and when his lips met hers, she didn't even notice the clapping and whistling that filled the hall and the door... the door that Cat never opens. But she is determined to conquer her fears as she's made new friends and wants to keep them. Then one night at a slumber party she finds that door... the door from her dreams, and the person behind it.

ZODIAC

*ARIES*TAURUS*GEMINI*CANCER*LEO*VIRGO*LIBRA*
*SCORPIO*SAGITTARIUS*CAPRICORN*AQUARIUS*PISCES*

Twelve signs of the Zodiac. Twelve novels, each one embracing the characteristics of a zodiac sign. Pushed to the extreme, these characteristics lead down twisting paths into tales of mystery, horror, romance and fantasy.

Whatever your sun sign, you will want to read Zodiac, the series written in the stars.

SERIES CREATED BY JAHNNA N. MALCOLM

AQUARIUS:

INDEPENDENT, INNOVATIVE
SECOND SIGHT

*A*mber has always been different. She discovers that she has special powers that frighten her. Her dreams about other people come true - with dramatic results. Can she really control other people's lives? Can she control her own? When disaster strikes at a rodeo, Amber's powers are put to the test.

SCORPIO:

PASSIONATE, FORCEFUL
DEATH GRIP

*S*abrina loves with a fierce intensity - even those who have died. First her mother drowns, and then Matt... Can *his* death really have been an accident or was it cold-blooded murder? Sabrina is determined to discover the truth - even if it means enlisting the help of a spirit from beyond the grave.

CAPRICORN:
PERSISTENT, AN ACHIEVER
DON'T LOOK BACK

*C*at is terrified. Her nightmares have returned. The house with the tiny staircase and the door… the door that Cat never opens. But she is determined to conquer her fears as she's made new friends and wants to keep them. Then one night at a slumber party she finds that door… the door from her dreams, and the person behind it.

CANCER:
EMOTIONAL, CARING
DARK SHADOWS

*C*hloe works tirelessly in her garden to create something beautiful, but nothing seems to flourish. Is it because a murderer used to live in the house before Chloe and her brother moved in? Then, a secret helper transforms the garden overnight – a secret helper who doesn't want Chloe to know his identity. Can the murderand the secret gardener be linked and can caring Chloe put the pieces of the chain together?